Staggering Through The Darkness

R. J. TIPTON

ISBN 979-8-89043-715-0 (paperback)
ISBN 979-8-89043-716-7 (digital)

Christian Faith Publishing
832 Park Avenue
Meadville, PA 16335
www.christianfaithpublishing.com

Printed in the United States of America

To all my brothers-in-arms, who continually fight the good fight of faith and preach the gospel of Jesus when you're overwhelmed, heartbroken, struggling to walk in repentance, dealing with the weight of the world on your shoulders, and just feel like you're spiritually bleeding to death. You are light in the darkness! Keep on shining!

To all the ministers who have fallen into depression and taken their lives. I wish I could've had a cup of coffee with you. My heart and prayers go out to all those who are left behind to pick up the broken pieces.

To anyone in the Body of Christ who can't seem to dig out of the sepulcher of shame, no matter how hard they try. May you realize today who you are in Jesus and live by His power through His grace and experience abundance.

Contents

Chapter 1

The Sweet Release from My Pain

My hands were sweaty and also shaking like a leaf wobbling in the wind as I looked down the barrel of the 9 mm pistol my daddy left me after he passed away from a lengthy fight with lung cancer. I affectionately referred to her as Black Betsy. He taught me how to shoot her, as well as many other firearms, but she was my favorite out of his entire arsenal. Hundreds of memories raced through my mind—memories that are so randomly weird, or at least mine seem to be.

Bits and pieces of my wedding day flashed through my mind like fireworks on the Fourth of July, along with the birth of each one of my kiddos and the moment their little eyes opened for the first time. I remember the cute formation of their lips, almost as if they were attempting to whistle for the nurse to hurry up and get the white gunk off of them. And let's not forget the hunting trips with my dad and my brother, filled with so much laughter as we all ribbed each other nonstop.

I also remember riding my little powder-blue Yamaha four-wheeler, imagining I was a famous NASCAR driver when I was just a ten-year-old boy. There was also an incident of punching some kid in the nose—I wish I could remember his name, but it has totally slipped my mind—all because I was totally fed up with him bullying little Scotty Ebert in the fourth grade. Then all of a sudden, I heard my dad saying so vividly, "Really? Are you really gonna blow your frigging brains out with my gun? C'mon, man!"

It might seem weird to you, but as soon as he asked this question, I began to laugh hysterically with the gun still pressed tightly to my forehead while the hammer was in the cocked position. This made my hand increasingly more unstable, to say the least, but was the transition I needed at the moment to allow the memories to pause for a minute or two while the mental interrogation began. You know what I mean by mental interrogation, don't you? If your dad served in the military like my old man, you probably get the gist. It's the barrage of questions that come out of nowhere like a tornado on a sunny day. Will I actually be able to pull the trigger this time, or will I try to talk myself out of it once again in my Dr. Phil head voice?

I probably haven't watched a full episode of *Dr. Phil* in my life, but my momma was always watching him, so it was like his voice was burned into my subconscious. Did I make sure I left the lid off the gun oil? Will it spill on the carpet? Crazy, huh? I'm contemplating splattering my brain matter everywhere, but I don't want to get a little gun oil on the carpet. Is the cleaning kit set up convincingly enough to make this look like another gun-cleaning accident instead of a premeditated suicide so my poor wife and five children could collect the money from my life insurance policy? Is it ethically wrong to do the insurance company that way? Did I make sure to remove the magazine from the gun after chambering a round?

I couldn't risk one of my smaller children finding me and accidentally hurting themselves with a semi-automatic handgun that was ready to fire another lethal bullet. What would my wife think? She was my high school sweetheart and the love of my life. We had an awesome marriage, really. Our twenty-fifth wedding anniversary was swiftly approaching, and we were planning to go back to Hawaii because that's where we spent our honeymoon. What would my children think? They are such good kids. I really don't know how they turned out with such good character and integrity. The eldest was getting ready to graduate from college, and his brother was getting ready to graduate from high school as the valedictorian of his private Christian school. My boys were always my buddies. I enjoyed hanging out with them. They both have such a good sense of humor and could always make me laugh, even through the worst situations.

My three girls absolutely adored me, and the feeling was mutual. I was always their hero, but I never really felt adequate enough to be viewed with such lofty admiration. The eldest girl is a freshman in high school and looks just like me. She is my brown-eyed girl. The next princess is an eighth grader and was affectionately called Red because she always had the shiniest, soft red hair. Last but not least was the baby of the family, who is now a sixth grader. Where has the time gone? She has always embraced the title of "Daddy's little fuzzy head" like a badge of honor. She would engage in hand-to-hand combat with Big Foot for her daddy. She has been spoiled absolutely rotten by everyone and doesn't even try to hide it. She just rolls with it.

Our family appeared to be the family that everybody wanted their families to be like. Our Facebook feed looked perfect the majority of the time. Most people's social media appears to look perfect, right? They normally just show the good and make it seem better than what it really is but would never let anyone get a glimpse of the bad or ugly. Honestly, my family is the only reason I haven't carried through with this sinister plot in my mind by now. Would the daddy that they adore so much be the one individual who hurts them the worst? Would they blame themselves? I love them with all of my heart, bigger than the sky and deeper than the ocean. But at this point, do I even really care what anyone would think anymore, including them? Should I leave a note or maybe a letter with some kind of explanation? Do I even have the strength to try to explain this? Would that just cause more questions to arise in their already broken hearts? Did I make sure to use the good ammo—you know, the hollow points designed to stop a home intruder, which should also make a big exit wound and finish the task at hand?

This is a much better choice for killing someone instead of using the cheap stuff you just shoot for fun at an empty Mountain Dew can on the farm, right? I mean, if I'm gonna be successful, I want to make sure it actually kills me. I've been successful in every other area of my life and even coach people on how to be successful in their lives, but would this be my epic fail? What if, instead of blowing a hole out the back of my head as big as a coffee mug, I fail? I mean, I could totally "screw the pooch," as Papaw used to say, when attempting to end my life, just leaving me in some vegetative state. Wouldn't that just be fantabulous, especially if I had consciousness in that state of just existing, which would be worse than hell itself, I suppose?

Well, I don't know if anything could compare to eternal damnation in a lake of fire, but I can only assume it would be a close runner-up. Just merely lying there with all of my thoughts running wild—the memories, the continual questions, the guilt, the shame, and the thoughts of what might have been. Oh, and let's not forget about the cravings—those dark, unstoppable, gnawing addictions that you can never truly run fast enough from or hide quietly enough to escape. What would my church family think? All the people I had preached to, prayed for, discipled, and counseled for more than twenty years. Oh yeah, I'm an ordained pastor by the way. I can only imagine the look on your face right now. Don't judge me, please. Well, maybe you should, and you even have a right to but only if it would make you feel better about yourself.

I know this is probably at least somewhat shocking to you because you might think ministers are subhuman superheroes, who wear real invisible capes and carry a Bible under their arm continually. They never really have a bad day, a bad thought, or slip up and say a dirty word. They're perfect or as close to perfect as you possibly can be. I hate to break it to you, but there are no perfect people in this world—zero, zilch, nada. Not even at your church, and no, not even your pastor is perfect. Even those ones you read about in the Bible, they aren't perfect either.

The authors of scripture had to be divinely inspired to write about their own rebellion and utter sinfulness. We wanna be the good guy in the story, but we are normally the villain—our very own worst enemy. Pastors and ministers are just ordinary people with an extraordinary call. They are limited, fallen, and sinners, who surrender their lives to glorify and magnify an unlimited, perfect savior. Even though I have already convinced you that I am flawed, please don't think I am condoning or excusing any of my actions. I am— without an excuse—just like you, as well as everybody else. We are totally responsible for our decisions.

You need to know that I'm not just any kind of pastor, mind you, but a fundamentalist—one of those *King James Bible* hell-fire-and-brimstone preaching, *Heavenly Highway Hymnal* singing, three-piece suit-and-tie-wearing Independent Baptists from the heart of the Bible Belt. I served in one of those churches that militantly encouraged its members to pass out tracts, actively go soul-winning, and schedule multiple all-day Bluegrass Gospel concerts throughout the year, which are always followed by dinner on the grounds.

One of those deals where everyone brings their favorite casserole dish, and there's bucket after bucket of fried chicken. It is one of those churches that prided themselves in the traditions of the fifties with a rule set so demanding that it would be impossible for Mary, the mother of Jesus, to actually keep. It was partly my fault because I instructed them with great zeal to be that way. Kinda weird, huh? Yep, I was totally faking it even though I didn't truly realize it at the time. I was just busy trying to get my life together while hoping that no one would ever find out what I was involved in or going through.

I was in a mess but felt stuck in the grave of hypocrisy I was continually digging for myself. They could never, under any circumstances, find out the truth. Why, you might ask. First and most importantly, it could hinder their walk with Christ and potentially stunt their spiritual growth. I know Christianity is about a real relationship with Jesus and not about ministry leaders, but my suicide would be so much more than just shocking to them that it would be life-altering. Secondly, and honestly, one of the most convincing reasons I was even contemplating taking my own life prematurely was the fact that these are the type of religious people who shoot their own wounded. What they viewed as holy, biblical standards, which separated them from the world, seemed like unloving exclusive spiritual elitism to those on the outside they were actually called to love and minister to. It felt like a performance-based competition for approval on the inside and became my responsibility not only to set the standard but live piously beyond them. I did it for my entire ministry.

Well, at least, I convinced them that I did anyways. Realistically, this church, which should've helped me work through my secret sins, would never accept me even though they expressed their love for me continually. If I opened up, became totally transparent about my mistakes, and aired my dirty laundry, it was game over. They would call one of those private business meetings, which their own bylaws prohibit, and kick me to the curb. Trying not to get caught or exposed is what caused me such mental anguish throughout the years. I couldn't be honest! My life was supposed to be about *truth*.

I could quote Jesus, "The truth shall make you free," in my fiery, southern preacher voice and get a thunderous round of applause and even a few hearty amens. However, the real truth is that you can put yourself immediately back into bondage just seconds after Jesus saves your soul. There is bondage in all kinds of forms, shapes, and sizes. Satan could care less which one you choose, as long as you choose one of them. Most people get trapped in the bondage of religion as soon as the gospel of Jesus sets them free. It is one of Satan's oldest tricks in the book, and people swallow the bait hook, line, and sinker. The real truth is there's a lifelong process of sanctification that every child of God must embark on and go through, and some people have a much messier journey than others.

Sanctification looks different for everyone. It sounds like false doctrine, especially to those who have a higher view of "church-ian-ity" than Christianity or if they are steeped in legalism. I know what you must be thinking right now and I get it: How does a radically conservative pastor, with more than twenty years of ministry experience, get to the potentially lowest point in their life to even contemplate suicide? It's a worthy question to ask, no doubt. It also deserves a truthful answer. Maybe, it would be better if I asked another question: What were the factors that led to staring down the barrel of a gun, or perhaps, why did I neglect my mental and emotional health for so long? By the way, just to make sure there's not any confusion, this was not one isolated event—I really wish it was.

You probably wouldn't think so badly of me if it was or maybe you would. You see, I thought about killing myself at least three or four times per week for longer than a year. It started with just a fleeting thought that comes outta nowhere—kinda like a squirrel darting across the road in front of your vehicle, barely escaping calamity, never to be seen again. And then it happens a week later, and you think to yourself, *Was that the same squirrel?* It's kinda like that but only heavier and much darker.

I went from wondering what would happen if I purposefully didn't turn as sharply as I should in a hairpin curve, which hopefully would slingshot me off the roadway to crash violently into a giant tree, to actually staring at my daddy's old pistol in some sort of a deep trance, while wondering how messy this would be for my wife to clean up and if she would end up hating me forever because of such a selfish act. I'm with you for sure—this totally sounds crazy. At least it would if I heard it from someone else. Actually, it always did seem so selfish to me when I heard these things from others. Believe it or not, I've counseled multiple suicidal people throughout my ministry, so I know the lingo. I know exactly what to say, but unsurprisingly, those words never made me feel any differently. They definitely don't make me feel any better.

As I would try to talk myself down, I would find myself drowning more in the ocean of my own hypocrisy and wallowing in the putrid sewer of my shame. I've asked myself over and over again, "How did I get here?" It's almost like a phrase that repeats itself over and over again from a scratched-up mid-nineties rap CD. The truth is that it didn't happen all in a day, but it was a slow drift that occurred day after day over the course of many years. You never truly understand the consequences of the bad decisions you are making in the initial stages, but the consequences really don't give a flip if you understand or can even process the severity of the damage. They just come out of nowhere, like a starving lion ready to devour you at the worst possible time.

This roller coaster consisting of my life has seen the highest of highs and lowest of lows. It has been able to scale beautiful mountain tops and fearfully and rather reluctantly navigate many dark, depressing, and lonely valleys. It's been the constant grappling between light and darkness, good and evil, righteousness and unrighteousness, holiness and depravity—like two grizzlies fighting over a plump salmon during a drought for their last meal. Guess what, I'm neither one of those grizzly bears but rather the battered remains of a half-dead fish, lying on the cold ground while barely breathing because of my wounds and not effectively claimed by either side. It seems like they both walk away after the confrontation, leaving me in this weird limbo between the spirit and the flesh. Spiritual warfare is a reality in the unseen realm.

Thankfully, Jesus never walks away and is willing to fight for us. I'm just being transparent by saying how it feels sometimes and how I kinda see it playing out in that world I can't see with my physical eyes. The initial conflict is violent and scary and can't end quickly enough, especially if you're the fish. The aftermath is less than satisfying because neither opponent ends up with the prize of a salmon supper, and the once frisky fish is now suffering a rather painful death for nothing. It seems brutally wasteful, doesn't it? This is how I feel after every struggle. I know the Bible says the Lord will never leave us or forsake us, but it surely doesn't feel that way through the seasons of our lives.

Jesus and Satan engaged in mortal combat over and over again for my peace, joy, and mental sanity; but it always left me feeling like wounded collateral damage afterward, just trying to find the energy to clean my emotional wounds and wiggle my way back to the water. It gets worse! Now imagine some tourist or nature enthusiast might stand at a safe distance and take multiple pictures of this showdown with their iPhone and refer to their experience by saying, "Dude, that was awesome!" But they are not referring to the duel between King Jesus and His sinister nemesis, Lucifer. Could you imagine posting that showdown on your social media accounts? Whoa! I'm talking about the fight for the salmon between the two bears.

The person who just so happens to capture this event kinda feels to me like all the people that I really don't know or who really don't know me either, just looking in on my life with a front-row seat because I am a public figure in our small, rural town. It kinda feels similar to dying a thousand deaths publicly on the town square. Everyone has their opinion, and everybody is going to willingly give you their opinion—free of charge, whether you ask for it or not. But very few know even half of the truth or even care to know the context. Either way, at least a suicide keeps me from facing them every day when the truth finally comes out and every secret is revealed. You might think I'm nothing more than a coward who is going to literally play the victim card, but honestly, I'm just tired of fighting. I am out of spiritual and emotional energy. I can't raise my hands at this point to attempt to protect myself from the multiple combinations coming my way from my spiritual enemy. When I pull this trigger, the war is finally over!

Chapter 2

Glory Days…or Were They?

My buddy, who just happened to be the tailback on our high school football team, said, "Dude, that was awesome! You are a total savage!" I'm sure my "eggs got scrambled" from the collision, which is the way we referred to a big hit or a good stick, because I can barely remember it to this day. It was the fourth quarter, with less than a minute left on the game clock; and the Admirals, our rivals, had the ball on the three-yard line, threatening to score.

It was fourth down, and I just so happened to move from the middle linebacker position—the position I played my entire senior year—to the outside linebacker position on the weak side because I made a split-second read of the offense's formation. I read it correctly because they ran a fake quarterback bootleg sweep. So for those of you who did not play football or have any fun with Madden on your gaming consoles, this play was a total misdirection to deceive the defense. You think the tailback is going to receive the handoff or a quick pitch from the quarterback as the play progresses to the right, but the quarterback fakes the pitch and rolls the other way, with the ball hidden behind his hip, for the easy touchdown. This is a great play to run if executed properly because the majority of the defenders are heading in the opposite direction.

Okay, enough with the Football 101 lecture. Well, the bootleg didn't work as they had anticipated it would on this night. As soon as the ball was snapped, I hit the tight end and the slot receiver with everything I had and won the inside position past one of their shoulders when out of nowhere, like a monster truck, the pulling guard—a big, usually fat, and normally intense lineman—plowed into my left knee. The cross collision from the lineman, coming one way to hit me below the waist and the tight end pushing me toward the point of impact from behind—launched my body violently into an aerial cartwheel, which was actually an exhilarating experience. I do remember that part, most definitely. The not-so-cool part of this story is that my knee popped like a rubber-band ball being exploded by an illegal Chinese firecracker.

If you didn't have as cool of a childhood as I did, you might not know what an M-80 is. First, let me apologize to you for your somewhat mostly lame upbringing. Secondly and most importantly, an M-80 was like a high-powered firecracker on steroids. Oh, the stories I could tell, but I will cautiously exercise a little self-control at this point. So what was so awesome about my knee getting utterly destroyed by what should have been an illegal block to the back but was never called by the ref that night? Believe it or not, I actually landed on my feet in a full sprint to run the quarterback down and make a shoestring tackle before he could break the plane of the goal line with the football.

Now you're probably thinking that I saved the game-winning touchdown. I wish it were true, but they were already beating us by a score of 72 to 0. Yeah, we were horrible that year, and they ended up playing in the state championship game at the conclusion of the season, only to lose by a last-second touchdown. I guess I really believe you should leave it all on the field and give your best effort to the last play, just like the coach had harped about all year long. However, I was in excruciating pain. The only pain worse than that experience was when the nerve block wore off after the surgery to totally replace my anterior cruciate ligament (ACL) and medial collateral ligament (MCL).

Recovery wasn't any fun at all, but I had hopes of playing some college football at a small school and needed to speed up the healing process. The more physical therapy I went through, the worse the pain got. Then the pain medication prescribed to me didn't last long enough, and it was weaker than what I thought I needed at the time.

It seemed like I went through them quickly because it had very little results in helping me manage my pain. I was prescribed Darvocet by my doctor with Tylenol 3. However, my old man took Vicodin, and according to him, Darvocet was like Michael Spinks and Vicodin was like Iron Mike Tyson. We all know how that ended up, don't we? In just ninety-one seconds, Tyson knocked Spinks into the shadow realm at the convention hall in Atlantic City, New Jersey.

I was convinced that I needed something vastly stronger than this weaker-than-water medication. I knew I had to do something because the pain was continually increasing; and the solution finally came to me one evening while I was sitting at the table eating supper, feeling sorry for myself, listening to a conversation between my parents. They were discussing how the Department of Veterans Affairs (VA) was going to increase the milligrams of Dad's pain medicine because his back and legs were getting worse. My old man served two tours in Vietnam as an army infantryman, where he severely injured his back. The longer he lived, the more pain he endured; and his doctors prescribed him pain pills, which he called "power pills" to help him cope with the continual pain.

I know what you're probably thinking again. I would probably be thinking the same thing at this point in the story too. Surely, you wouldn't do that to your own father, would you? Yeah, I did! I stole some of his "Tyson Power Punch Pills" without his knowledge but not that night. It took me a few days or so, maybe even a week, to justify it in my mind. Goodness gracious, he's my dad, so you know he wouldn't mind, right? He loves me and wouldn't want to see me in pain. Also, he would want me to progress in my recovery faster so I could potentially play football at the collegiate level. It was something I had dreamed of ever since kindergarten when I suited up for the Castlewood Cowboys in the peewee division. He would probably expect me to take them and think it would be silly to even ask him. I wouldn't even need that many of them anyways, you know, just enough to get me through this PT, which should be called *pain* and *torture* instead of physical therapy, to begin with.

It wouldn't be any different than eating one of his beloved oatmeal creme pies, right? He wouldn't mind at all! So I got up late in the night about a week later and miraculously made it to the kitchen, as quietly as I possibly could on crutches, and finally located the cabinet with the medicine. I could barely see because I was too big of a chicken to turn on the light. My dad awakened easily and got up multiple times through the night because of his increasing pain level. I couldn't risk him catching me. What would I say? How would he react when he discovered his son, his fishing and hunting buddy, was stealing his pain medication? I was thoroughly convinced in my mind that I didn't want to experience his wrath. He was a trained soldier and didn't have the temperament to be stolen from even by his own son. Actually, that look of disgust from his disappointment in my actions would by far supersede any of his military training being unleashed on me even though I would probably be deserving of it.

I opened the door to the cabinet, and the hinge squealed louder than any rooster's crow I'd ever heard. I'm thinking to myself, *Well, it's inevitable now. I'm gonna get caught for sure.* I waited for about twenty seconds, standing in the darkness, which seemed like an hour before I tried to somewhat blindly feel my way around for the pill bottle. There was just a glimmer of light coming from a lamp reflecting off a mirror in the room, adjoining the kitchen. I felt the rough edges of the lid on the pill bottle on the tip of my fingers, but I was having a difficult time getting a firm grip on it. In an attempt to scoot closer to the counter on my crutches, I lost my balance and crashed to the floor, like a beached whale crashing onto the beach shore or kinda like spinks crashing to the canvas from that powerful uppercut.

All of a sudden, I heard the very distinct voice of my dad echoing down the hallway like the former drill sergeant he used to be saying, "Hey, are you okay? What the h——l are you doing?" I'm trying to spare you from cusswords because remember, I'm a preacher. By the time I tried to give a quick answer, his ominous shadow was looming over me. He helped me up and scolded me for being too hardheaded to ask for help. He said, "You're going to end up messing up your other leg, you knucklehead."

I didn't confess my motives, ashamedly. I told him that I was in too much pain to get any rest. At that point, I couldn't even make eye contact with him, which was a very big deal to him during communication. He said, "I tell you what, the VA just give me some new pain pills. They don't totally take away the pain, but they take enough of the sharpness of the pain away that they might help you sleep. You better not tell your momma or I will break my foot off in a place that wasn't designed for a foot! Do you understand?"

I shook my head, affirming that I understood, with a demur grin on my face. I just wanted to come clean and tell him what I was really doing in the kitchen, but I couldn't bring myself to do it, knowing it would disappoint him greatly. He unscrewed the lid from the bottle and dumped a few of the little white pills out in his hand. He dropped half of a Vicodin tablet into my palm as he turned his scuffed-up hand over on top of mine and got me a swig of water from the faucet on the sink. Of course, I swallowed it because that was the intended goal from the beginning of my failed pill heist. I slept better than I had slept since the surgery even through the pain of the newly placed titanium screw holding my ligaments in place to make my knee football functional again, hopefully. I did not expect what happened next. After my momma helped me get ready for school because I needed all the help I could get after my knee surgery, she drove into town with the old man that morning. I didn't ask why. I was just waiting for one of my friends to pick me up for school. He was running late as usual but demanded to take me because he was convinced that his humble act of compassionate service for me would get him more attention from some cheerleaders. Goodness, everyone needs a friend like that, huh?

Most postpubescent young men seem to do a lot of strange things to attract the attention of the ladies during their last couple years of high school. While waiting rather impatiently and before I even tried to rationalize it, I had already taken three pills out of Daddy's pill bottle and put them in my pocket. The still small voice in my head instructed me to put them back, but I refused with what seemed like hundreds of justifiable reasons to keep them safe and secure in my pocket. Was I already addicted? I don't know for sure, but I was heading in a dangerous direction. I didn't repeat this process every day but frequently enough to have an intense moment with both of my parents as the month came to an end. You see, I didn't think that my two or three pills here, and there would ever catch up to me, but was I wrong? Granny was right when she said, "It'll all come out in the wash, honey. It always does!"

I never knew what that meant as a little fella, but it seemed like I was caught in the high-speed spin cycle when I arrived home after school that day. It was a beautiful winter day; as a matter of fact, it didn't seem like winter at all. You could hear me approaching more than a mile away. The six sub woofers in the bed of my Mazda low-rider totally took away my element of surprise and that's the way I liked it. By this time, I wasn't working to increase my forty-yard dash speed, but I was managing to walk in a knee brace without the help of those stupid crutches. I hated those things! I strolled into the house, to the best of my ability, sporting my letterman jacket while wearing my new Jordans. It was a good day, or at least it was, before the confrontation.

The sun was shining, and I was feeling good. Not to mention, a buddy at school gave me some Vicodin that belonged to his mother, without her permission, of course. They were prescribed to her from a previous surgery, and she had recovered, so it was a win-win for me. Not so fast, when I opened the door and entered the kitchen, both of them were waiting for me at the table. We didn't even exchange a greeting. They said, "Sit down at the table and tell us the truth!" Daddy realized that he was missing pills when he ran out of them well before the month was over. He was prescribed three per day and took them exactly like his doctor told him to. This had turned into a math equation at this point, and it just didn't add up. To complicate things even more, he was extremely irritable because he was in a bunch of pain, which made me feel absolutely horrible. He didn't know whether he should tell his doctor or not because he didn't know if he could get in trouble. He was concerned that he might be accused of selling them at the worst or overmedicating himself at least. At the time, Health Insurance Portability and Accountability Act (HIPPA) policies were just introduced; and in our small town, it wouldn't matter much because it would be next to impossible to enforce it anyways.

Everybody knew everything about everybody's business, including the latest juicy gossip. I can only imagine how bad it would've been if social media was accessible at the time. The only social media around back then took place at the local barbershop by "Terry Talks Too Much" and in the hair salon by "Bertha Big Mouth and Slanderous Sally." Of course, those weren't really their real names, but they might as well have been.

"Well, do you know what happened to them? Please tell me you didn't take them! Why are you being so quiet?"—the questions kept coming like they were being shot out of a fire hose. I really wanted to tell the truth. I wanted to be brave and just own up to my selfish thievery, but I just couldn't. Do you know the difference between the reaction of a herd of wild buffalo and domesticated cattle when a storm is brewing in the area? The buffalo stop immediately in their tracks and carefully investigate the sky to determine where the storm is located and in what direction the storm is heading. Then surprisingly, they run in the opposite direction you would expect them to, which is straight into the eye of the storm. As a result, the storm passes them quickly because they meet it head-on and bravely travel through it. On the other hand, a herd of cattle will run away from the storm, which just happens to be the same direction the storm is traveling. It takes a little longer to get to them, but they end up enduring the worst of the storm for much longer periods because they react in fear and run along the same path with the storm frantically. Sometimes, animals, even wild animals, exercise more wisdom than humans do, unfortunately. I was not like a brave buffalo in this scenario. I made a split-second decision to run with the storm like a cowardly cow, foolishly thinking I was escaping the flashing lightning, the golf ball–sized hail, and the rolling thunder. Have you ever been there? If so, just go ahead and take a short pause in your reading to moo like a cow. *Moo!*

The only thing I could come up with as a response to the heavy questioning by my parents was to blame the mysterious shortage on my crazy cousins. Everybody has a few of them, right? If you can't think of who they are in your family, just realize it could be you. You very well might be the crazy cousin in your family. It seemed to work!

They both turned their attention from me and grabbed the phone to dial my aunt, the mother of those crazy cousins, who was just as crazy—if not crazier—as all of her children combined. They denied it—and rightfully so—because they were innocent; but my parents just knew they were lying. *It* serves the hoodlums right for all the drama they caused me during my childhood. The only thing any of them would amount to would be inmates in some state penitentiary anyways.

This was just an allegation that couldn't be proven. It wasn't like we had a camera system for security in our country home. Besides, they already had much worse stuff on their arrest records. There were only a couple of them, on that side of the family, that made anything out of themselves besides felons. We were different than them even though folks knew they were our kinfolk, or were we really any different at all? Maybe Momma and Daddy were, but was I really any different? Only time would truly tell, and I had great ambitions and big goals—way too big for this Podunk, poke and plumb town.

You know what a poke-and-plumb town is, don't you? You poke your head around the corner, and you're plumb out of town. Yep, it was that small. Momma never connected the dots by tracing the mystery of the missing medication back to me—well, not until years later after I had the accident. Nope, not my football injury, but the event that will always be referred to as "the accident" by the folks closest to me.

Chapter 3

The Accident

By now, several years passed, and I was happily married to my high school sweetheart. And we were excited to start a family. Life was coming at us quickly. We both graduated from a private Christian college, and guess what? I didn't play football. Surprisingly, I didn't even really want to but would've certainly made the roster and probably would have received plenty of playing time at this smaller school that had a struggling program at the time. I really didn't want to take the chance of blowing my knee out once again either. I had thoughts of playing professional football as a kid. What kid doesn't dream of being a professional athlete one day? However, those pep talks our Momma gave us aren't always true, are they? You really can't do anything you set your mind to or be anything you want to be through hard work.

I'm a little aggravated at Hulk Hogan too because I was a Hulk-a-maniac growing up, who said my prayers, ate my veggies, and kept on believing that I would play for the Cincinnati Bengals one day. Sure, I was a decent athlete in high school but not good enough to be considered a D-1 or even a D-2 athlete in college—much less, a professional football player. That dream died just like so many dreams do when they have a face-to-face run-in with reality. There were only two things on my mind during my college years: getting married and preaching the Gospel. It totally consumed me. I maintained a 3.5 GPA while preaching three weeks out of the month of my entire junior and senior year, which was pretty impressive for me, considering I wasn't the best student in high school.

My motto was, "C's get degrees!" It seemed like every night I was the evangelist at a different revival meeting or youth conference. I would drive more than an hour one way to preach during the evening, drive back to school, and stay up half the night to study for tests and write papers. Needless to say, coffee became my friend at this time. It's a good thing energy drinks weren't really popular yet. I couldn't imagine drinking Monsters like I drank coffee. I was united in holy matrimony to the love of my life a couple months after graduation. She was beautiful, absolutely stunning on our wedding day. I will never forget the moment when those double doors opened in that little country church, the music began to play, and she began her elegant stroll down the center aisle with her father. I almost immediately begin serving as the pastor of a small congregation out in the boonies in rural Kentucky after the wedding.

We spent our honeymoon years engulfed in ministry work and enjoyed each other's companionship. We were madly in love with each other. She was my best friend, and she made me believe that I could accomplish anything in the world at that time. A couple of years later, we had our first baby boy. Wow! What a humbling experience to be a father! The overwhelming sense of pride, gratitude, nervousness, and responsibility hits you all at the same in the center of the chest, like an arrow shot from a bow when you hold that baby for the first time. It was one of the most wonderful blessings I had ever received. So at this point, you undoubtedly have some questions for me. What about the opioid cravings? Did your wife know about your addiction? How did you go from stealing your daddy's Vicodin and lying like a dog about it to preaching revivals, pastoring a local church, and being a family man? I know, I've got some explaining to do right about now.

The simplest and most profound way to answer these lingering questions is by giving you a name—Jesus. He was the answer to all of my questions and the solution to all of my problems. He saved me in the summer—between the completion of my senior year of high school and before I enrolled in college as a freshman—and called me to the ministry almost immediately. Whether you believe it now or not, you could have waterboarded me, starved me, and beat me continuously; and you still couldn't have convinced me that King Jesus didn't have His hand on me at the time.

My life was radically changed! I was delivered from the prison of my past and forgiven of all my lying, cheating, stealing, and rebellion by his marvelous grace. The good news of the gospel seemed extra good to me in my depraved condition. It was a "Damascus Road Experience," just like the one we read about in the Bible that transformed Saul from a deacon-murdering and church-hating persecutor of Christians to the apostle Paul—a church-planting, gospel-preaching missionary. I was ultimately convinced that God totally eradicated the craving and the continual gnawing I had developed for pain pills at that time, but nothing could be further from the truth. I'm not saying that God can't totally take those addictions away or that He doesn't totally take them away for some people. He is God, and He does what He pleases. One thing is for sure, during that season of my life, it was like I was walking with Him hand in hand. It was a blessed season for growth in ministry, and even though it was busy, I was enjoying every minute of it.

I just flew back home from a big youth conference in another state where I had preached five sermons in two days. I was totally worn out, but I couldn't wait to get some much-needed therapy on my Harley. Some guys play golf, but the grounds keepers don't mow where I usually hit my ball, so it's not one of those outlets that I can enjoy as some fellas do. The few times I have attempted to play, I have left the country club more frustrated than leaving a church business meeting to discuss the annual budget. It could be because I am extremely competitive or that those types of meetings just totally "suck an egg," in my pastoral opinion. That's the phrase my circle of ministry *compadres* would often use to refer to something they didn't want to do but was expected of them in their . ministerial duties.

Yep, some things about ministry—"suck an egg"—and if you had to oversee and moderate one of these budgeting meetings, I am certain you would say the same thing. Who really cares how much toilet paper we use or how much money we spend on Goldfish Crackers to feed the children in the nursery? I really don't think God cares how much we wipe our booties or about the consumption of snacks for our children's ministries; and even if he does, why do we have to have a two-hour meeting about it, right? Inevitably, there would always be some "Karen," who just so happens to catch a fifty-seven cent mathematical error and then develops some grand conspiracy of money laundering in her mind, which now exists as a state of emergency that we must address for the next fifteen minutes. I would be willing to contribute a dollar to solve this crisis just to ease her spidey senses, but it never really makes them happy. Why? Because now there's a forty-three-cent surplus and we are still out of budget, right? Please don't be a "Church Karen"; even though every church just has to have one, it doesn't have to be you. Is it really worth the time or the energy for such a grand amount of less than twelve dollars over the next twenty years? Nope! C'mon y'all! Good gravy! Let's keep the main thing, the main thing. Let's focus on Jesus!

I had a shiny metallic blue Harley Davidson Softtail Fat Boy Cruiser that was used as my mental break from these types of stressful times in life. Honestly, I didn't have to be stressed to ride it. Stress was just another excuse to ride it. There's just something about riding that I can't really explain. If you know, you know. Where would I go? Who knows? But I couldn't wait to get out of those uncomfortable churchy clothes, throw on some jeans and a hoodie, and hit the open road. The parkway was absolutely stunning. I really wanted to open Blue Betsy up, but I decided to just cruise in the slow lane instead. It was fall, my favorite time of the year; and all the leaves were changing colors on the trees, saturating the cliffs surrounding the lake. I was just taking it all in. The catchy tune of "It's A Great Day to Be Alive" by Travis Tritt was playing on repeat over and over in my head. My heart was overflowing with God's goodness in my life. I was thinking about my beautiful wife, my baby boy who had just started crawling around and jabbering like a Pentecostal preacher filled with the Holy Ghost, and the awesome opportunities for the ministry God had entrusted to me. Everything seemed perfect, just like the jaw-dropping scenery around me. Little did I know that my life was getting ready to change just like those multi-colored leaves on the trees I was beholding.

Those beautiful orange, copper, and rusty-red leaves would soon lose their vibrancy and fall to the ground just in another month or so as winter set in. My life would literally come crashing down, as well as a few more miles up the road, just like falling leaves scattered on the ground. Life is full of surprises, isn't it? For years everything can seem to run smoothly, and then all at once, everything can change in a split second. I was waiting patiently at the stoplight, heading into town after cruising to the closest city nearby, which was about thirty minutes from my house. I was first in line, in my lane at the intersection, awaiting the green light to set me free like a professional drag racer. The metal flake in the metallic blue paint was glistening in the sun as Blue Betsy was impeccably clean. As soon as the light turned green, I eased off the clutch and gave the throttle a little torque. She purred halfway through the intersection when I heard the explosion.

I really don't remember what happened other than filling in the bits and pieces by family, friends, and the EMS first responders who worked the scene of the wreck. This one was not as graceful as the football tackle even though it was aerobatic. I didn't land on my feet to chase down an agile quarterback. As a matter of fact, I wouldn't stand on my feet for a few months as I lay flat on my back in a hospital bed. I was told afterward that a teenager, who was driving a new Jeep Wrangler way too fast, didn't notice the red light because she was texting and driving. I always wanted a new Jeep Wrangler but never could afford one. Those things are too expensive, in my opinion. I chose the Harley over the Jeep, and I'm glad I did. I was glad at the time of the purchase anyways. If you ever get stuck in making a decision between the two, just go ahead and select the motorcycle. You won't regret it, and you'll thank me for it later—guaranteed. Well, you won't regret it unless you get run over by a chick in a Jeep like I did.

At that point, you might potentially wish you had purchased the Wrangler instead if you survive the crash by the grace of God. The crazy thing is, I wouldn't recognize that girl if she walked up and introduced herself to me. I heard that she ended up overdosing on meth years later. What a loser! Just kidding! I got ya good, didn't I? I really don't know how she turned out or if she even lived around here. Hopefully, she learned to be more responsible while driving and has enjoyed a prosperous life. I have no hard feelings toward her at all. She was just a kid, probably enjoying the day just like I was up until the crash. I actually pray for her from time to time. Thankfully, she had good insurance or my insurance company had better lawyers than her insurance company did because I got a decent settlement out of the accident. I never got to enjoy any of the money. It was enough, however, to pay my medical bills, which was a burden lifted off our minds.

The accident definitely changed my life. It changed my wife's life too. I will never forget that terrified look on my wife's face—the alligator tears welled up in her eyes and the sigh of relief she exhaled tiredly when she finally made eye contact with me after it took me more than three weeks to open my eyes and respond to commands. I was in bad shape medically, but I was alive. I had multiple surgeries and a very long and painful road of recovery ahead of me. May I just pause for a praise break to thank the Lord for morphine and ice chips? There were so many people who visited me the first week that the hospital had to turn some newly renovated office space into waiting rooms just to accommodate the growing crowd. They were singing, praying, and bringing my wife so many cakes, cookies, and pies that we could have opened a bakery. Country folks can be backward at times and downright confrontational if you trespass on their land even if it's an accident, but I am convinced that they are the best people on this old mud-ball planet. I could be biased and somewhat uninformed in my opinion because I haven't been around to many high-fluting city folks.

After the first week, the calls and texts were overwhelming for her. She just could not keep up with them fast enough. All those people who showed up with deserts, prayed, and continued to check on me daily through text messages would never understand the darkness I would stumble through over the next few years. Isn't that what life is kinda like? We are all a mess just stumbling through the darkness in this old world while trying to keep our eyes on Jesus, who stands as a light house in our helplessness. Sometimes, we look in His direction, and He is easily seen. But then at other times, we don't seem to even know what direction to look as we spin frantically out of control just trying to get a glimpse of that light. We walk by faith and not by sight, according to the Bible. But on some days, our walk kinda resembles an old drunk man just staggering through the darkness, if we are being honest with ourselves. Speaking of walking and stumbling, I had to learn how to do that all over again.

My baby boy was now pulling up and taking steps. It was not only precious but encouraging. I looked just like him, taking one unbalanced and awkward step after the other with the aid of my physical therapists. Instead of him following my example, I followed his example, and we learned how to walk together. It was kinda comical on most days and just downright frustrating on others. I wanted to give up multiple times and just order me a Hoveround, but I kept fighting. My little guy would clap his little hands and cheer for me by saying, "Yay and good job, Daddy," which sounded more like "goo jah Dahdi" when he said it. Sometimes I wondered if he realized how much I needed the coaching and the positive affirmations. Hospital life was starting to feel normal, kinda like I would be in there for the rest of my life. The staff was so amazing that it felt like home in a weird sort of way. My granny used to say, "It's amazing what we can get used to. What some folks consider normal." The next season of my life would prove her statement to be true.

Chapter 4

The Dark Revival of an Old Craving

The recovery was long and hard, but I finally got to where I could enjoy normal activities. I mean, I wasn't squatting, deadlifting, or power cleaning like I used to in the weight room back in high school, preparing for the Friday night lights. I wasn't planning on running a marathon either. I had already made up my mind and would stick to my guns by saying, "No thank you," when asked if I wanted to play a game of pickup basketball with some of the teenagers from our church.

Life seemed to go back to normal for everyone really, but me. I looked normal once again, like my old self, but there was a war raging on the inside of me. This war was fought on the battlefield in my mind—one grueling battle after the next, over every single choice I had to make, whether positive or negative, to try to manage my pain. I was in pain all the time. I couldn't just sit or lie down and ever get comfortable. It took a toll on me mentally and emotionally, but I kept putting on my smile and tried to stay positive. I was taking Ibuprofen and Tylenol 3 as the doctor recommended and still endured pain. My goal, at that time, was to try to stay away from the stronger narcotic pain pills. I was irritable, kinda like my old man, and didn't even realize it.

Finally, I went to a pain clinic for a consultation with a doctor that came highly recommended to me. He seemed like a great guy who really cared about his patients. We hit it off instantly because not only did he play college football but he was also a huge Bengals fan. We talked about our families, hunting, ministry, and football, of course. He didn't seem to be in any kind of rush even though the lobby was packed and the phone was ringing off the hook. He told me that life was too short and my calling was too important to just try to push through the pain. I will never forget the next words spoken by my new friend, "I'm gonna prescribe you OxyContin. They're much better than the Vicodin your daddy used to take, and they are far less likely to be addictive."

Okay, this is the best of both worlds. I can manage my pain more efficiently and don't have to worry about getting hooked on these pills. He recommended starting by taking three pills per day as needed. I couldn't wait to get home and tell my wife. I could see the light at the end of the tunnel and she would be so thankful. My appointment was in the afternoon, and I had to get back to my office for a counseling session. I never minded counseling struggling couples, but sometimes, I just wanted to look at them and say, "Quit being selfish! Schedule more date nights! Have as much fun as possible while making up after each fight."

Everything else will work itself out if only it were that easy. Satan desires to destroy families, and I would've been utterly shocked on that cloudy afternoon if you told me that he was getting ready to use my old habits to attack my family like never before. You see, a revival was getting ready to take place—not the one we had been praying for, not the one we hoped to see spread through our churches and turn the heart of our nation back toward God. This was a revival of something I thought was dead, but it wasn't. The craving was just lying there like a menacing dragon, who had been locked away in a dungeon to keep the villagers safe from harm in some fable or a children's storybook. God forbids us to awaken this beast to breathe his destructive fire once again.

I was stumbling through the darkness to revive this dragon inside of me, and I didn't even realize it. I headed to the pharmacy as soon as they opened the next morning and took my first OxyContin, which was prescribed by my new BFF and pain doctor. I really didn't notice much difference until almost a week later. I was feeling better, or at least, I thought I was. However, it didn't take long before my three pills per day turned into three and a half and then went to four pills. My addiction to pills grew like the crescendo in an auctioneer's voice as he called out the bid and compelled his audience for more and more, just one more bid, in his attempt to get the most out of an item up for sale. I don't even want to think about the first time I ran out of my prescribed pills in the middle of the month.

It was obviously noticeable to my wife as I was complaining about being in pain when she compassionately sprang into action by going to the cabinet to get me a pain pill. When she picked up the empty bottle, a weird and rather confused look came over her face. Here we go, the game of one thousand questions has just begun, and I am in the hot seat. That still small voice was telling me to tell the whole truth and nothing but the truth, and I totally blew it. My wife had never lied to me, to my knowledge, but the truth was not reciprocated. The guilt rushed in like a tidal wave from a tsunami. I actually blamed it on my old man in a roundabout way.

"You know, he had to have medication and had been taking them for years, so I gave him one of my pills, and he said they helped him so much more than his medication. He was running short, so I gave him some of mine, not really thinking what kind of a pickle that would leave me in." She bought it! I totally convinced her, but I could see this mental picture of Jesus shaking his head at me in disappointment—maybe, more than just disappointment but divine disgust. He shed His precious blood on the old rugged cross to purchase my salvation, but He wasn't really getting what he paid for. I was ripping Him off with the choices I made and was continuing to lose battle after battle in my mind. I guess, I kinda understood how Peter felt after he denied Him the third time.

Could you imagine locking eyes with Jesus after just denying that you were one of his disciples multiple times? Maybe you can't, but I know what that feels like, to my shame. I also know what it feels like to suffer through the withdrawal of not having OxyContin in my system. My body was crying out for help with each self-inflicted symptom I had to endure. The diarrhea and nausea weren't any fun, but the chills and insomnia were the worst. I couldn't really do anything but stare a hole through the ceiling while lying wide awake in the bed with feverish chills that just wouldn't quit while pooping on myself multiple times through the night. There wasn't any way I could make it to the bathroom in time. I felt like I was losing control of my life, right along with my sanity.

I couldn't keep from thinking back to when I stole my daddy's pills and ran him short on his medication for the month. Did he also just suffer silently through these horrible symptoms? How could I do such a selfish and horrible thing to someone I loved so much? The shame was almost unbearable. My poor little wife was so naive to all of this craziness going on around her. She had no idea what withdrawal symptoms looked like, so she started a prayer chain in her ladies' group at church because she was convinced I had a nasty stomach bug.

Could I make it until my prescription is refilled? At this rate, probably not. She finally called my new doctor and told him the truth. He sincerely apologized to her and increased my prescription frequency from three pills a day to four pills a day, and he also increased the strength of the dosage after consulting with me during my next office visit. This seemed like the solution but was literally worse than putting a Band-Aid on a heart attack. I really don't think he even realized the severity of my addiction. He seemed to be trying to help me out. Surely, four "Foxy-Cottons" per day, as my daddy called them, would be the answer to my prayer. I went from singing "Jesus, Take the Wheel" by Carrie Underwood, which was the most popular song on the radio at the time to praying, "Jesus, fill my pills, give them to me now, cause I can't make it on my on."

This was my dark reality. Do you think this really solved my problem? Nope, it didn't because I started taking four pills as prescribed, and then it quickly increased to five per day. Pretty soon, I got stuck in the same place again, going through the same withdrawal symptoms, but now my wife was starting to wisen up to the reality of what was going on. I had to do something, right? So I reached out to my crazy cousins. You might not remember me mentioning them earlier, but they were the ones who got blamed for my old man's missing pills back in high school. I was brutally honest with them because I was as desperate as I had ever been before in my life. They connected me with some sketchy-looking hillbilly, who called me on my landline at the church office and would only meet with me if I agreed to a private location that he got to choose.

He informed me that the going rate on the street for Oxy was seven dollars per pill, at the time; but he had to have twelve dollars because this was just too risky, according to him. He didn't want to violate his probation and get thrown back in the slammer. I asked him how many he was willing to sell, and he said he could probably part with fifty of them rather reluctantly. I could tell he was really nervous and didn't really trust me, so it probably didn't help to improve our rapport when I pulled out my checkbook and asked him, "To whom should I make the check out?" He said, "Really, you gotta be frigging kidding me, man! I ain't taking no check from you! You think this is the grocery store or something? I ain't telling you my real name, and I ain't taking no d——n check. It's cash or nothing!"

Well, this just got more complicated. Life is just that way, isn't it? The bank was closed, and the most I could withdraw from the ATM was $400. Good gravy! Nothing was going right with my first drug deal transaction. I just pictured it going a whole lot smoother in my mind. Maybe, God was intervening to stop me from making such a ridiculous decision. He said he was only waiting fifteen minutes and then he was leaving. The clock was ticking in my head.

Ironically, I pulled out in front of a Ninja stunt bike on my way out of the bank. Go figure! He almost wrecked but kept his bike upright and commenced, giving me the worst cussing I ever received in my life. I waved sheepishly to say I was sorry, and he returned the wave by flipping me off. I guess, I deserved it. I pulled back into our discreet location at a high rate of speed on two wheels in my Toyota Camry. I hesitantly informed him that I could only withdraw $400 from the ATM and began the used car salesman-type negotiation by promising the dude that if he would cut me a deal just this one time, I would give him $14 per pill from here on. This would be an additional $100 per month for him and his family. I was trying to be a blessing! He agreed and pulled the medicine bottle out of the back pocket of his Wrangler jeans.

I ignorantly reached for his bottle when he said, "Let me guess, you ain't even got nothin' to put 'em in do ya?"

I replied, "I have never done this before. Can you tell I'm a newbie?"

He said, "No s———t, Sherlock," and some other profanities, while dumping the Oxy out in my hands as he shook his head in aggravation.

I got back in the car and immediately popped a pill, chewing it up like an Altoid Mint because I didn't have anything to drink with me in the car. I don't know if there's any science backing this hypothesis, but the Oxy seemed to be more potent if you just chewed it up like a piece of candy. Maybe, it was just in my head, but it really didn't matter to me. I was convinced. It didn't take me too long to get past the nasty, bitter taste that went along with chewing the medication instead of swallowing it with the drink of my choice.

Murphy's Law proved to be active in the series of setbacks I had encountered throughout the day, and I really didn't even believe in Murphy's Law. But it proved to be a blessing in the long run because the dude told my cousin that he refused to meet with me anymore. He said I scared him, which made me laugh. To think this guy was scared by the likes of me was humorous. The plan for the future would work like a two-way street as he agreed to deliver the pills to my cousin, and she would be responsible for collecting his money from me when I picked up the next month's supply. Sounds great! I love it when a plan comes together.

On the other hand, $700 per month is a lot of money for a pastor of a mid-sized congregation when considering the rest of my bills also had to be paid. I was always instructed to pay my bills in a timely fashion by older, wiser ministers to keep from ruining my testimony and losing my influence. I wonder how people would avoid me if they really knew what I was doing. I knew it was illegal but justified it just like I did when it came to taking more medication than prescribed by my doctor. The new line item in the family budget would remain a secret, but just think, I could've bought myself a sharp Jeep Wrangler for sure with that kind of monthly payment.

It's amazing what we can justify, isn't it? I was becoming a pro at what I called "justification protocol," especially when it came to keeping a good supply of Oxy on hand. The biggest obstacle was attempting to successfully hide this from my wife. She kept track of our account like an IRS auditor. I had to think of something because I just couldn't imagine going through those hideous withdrawals again. It had certainly been an eventful evening. I was exhausted and just wanted to go home and get in bed. By the time I walked through the door like a paranoid zombie, the medication was kicking in. Oh yeah! I will rest like a baby tonight and not have to worry about the chills from the withdrawals that almost chattered my teeth out of my mouth.

When I made it to the end of the hallway and entered the bedroom, my wife was sitting on the edge of the bed, weeping with her head planted in her hands. She was on to me! I was getting ready to get busted. My goose was cooked. Even though my heart was racing and my adrenaline kicked in, I was almost relieved that the truth was finally going to come out. She would be the only person in my life who could truly help me fight this addiction.

She said, "Listen, I really need to talk to you! I don't know how this could've happened. I don't know what we are going to do?"

I just immediately began to apologize unspecifically and told her that I loved her so much, through my cracking voice and tear-filled eyes. We were going to make it through this by the grace and power of God. The preacher came out in me as I said, "If He can part the Red Sea, get the three Hebrew boys out of the fiery furnace without a single singed hair on their heads, or deliver Daniel from the lion's den, then He can get us through this."

She nodded her head and said, "That's one of the reasons I love you so much. You always know exactly what to say and you have so much faith."

It's just like time froze when she made that statement, and I had an out-of-body experience at that moment, which wasn't really the refreshing break from my hypocrisy that I needed. She really believes I have great faith. Wow! I was just scratching my head in confusion on that one. If she only knew the doubts that gripped my heart and paralyzed me emotionally. I continually begged God over and over to take this gnawing addiction away from me and keep me from staggering on through the darkness for so long that I have become numb. My faith doesn't seem to be helping me, and I am convinced that this hopelessness will be the sad dilemma of my somewhat wasted life. That doesn't sound like faith at all to me. How about you?

To me, I wrestled daily with what sounded like me already giving up and just submitting repeatedly to the control of my addiction. I was mentally and emotionally tapped out. I snapped back to reality after hearing her repeat this question to me for the second time: "So do you think this one will be a boy or a girl? Are you listening to me?"

There was an awkward silence, and I don't really even remember my reply, but I'm sure I did. It was probably only some muttering confusion, which prompted her to make the announcement. "I'm pregnant! Are you excited about it?"

She was pregnant! The sheer bliss of realizing I hadn't been busted at that time was more exciting to me than finding out I would become a father again for the second time. The dark revival was successful in accomplishing its intended goal. I was an addict. My craving and somewhat crippling addiction were alive and stronger than I could've ever imagined it could be. Things just got darker from here on—much darker. Our eyes can deceive us in the darkness, can't they? You flip the light switch off at bedtime, only to stumble across the room to your bed. You do this over and over—again and again, night after night—but you still stump your toe or bust your shinbone on the bed frame from time to time. However, after you lay there for a few minutes trying to let your mind gear down, you realize it was not as dark as it was just five minutes ago, or at least, it doesn't seem to be.

You can actually look around and see things now that you couldn't quite make out before. Has the darkness changed? Has it lessened? No, absolutely not. Your eyes have just adjusted to the darkness, which helps us to feel more relaxed and comfortable in the dark. The same thing is true in many of our lives. We get to a point where we feel way too relaxed in the dark, which just leads us into deeper and deeper darkness. Self-deception is a painfully pitiful way to live. This was the definition of my life at this point. I was also a pro at deceiving myself while I lived to point others to the truth. The dark revival wasn't over just yet, it was only just beginning.

Chapter 5

A New Door for a Different Craving

A revival is an awakening for believers to help them identify areas where they need to be more Christlike, which should help them to make the most of their daily lives by taking every opportunity to advance the kingdom of God as they take up their individual crosses to fulfill the pending task of the Great Commission. To say it in a much less churchy way, we need to be the hands, hearts, and feet of Jesus until He returns to intentionally love people where they're at and serve them. That's why the church exists, right?

Sometimes, we get consumed with the cares of this life and need to refocus and reprioritize the most important things so we don't live for a lesser name than the name of Jesus. This is good, wholesome, and necessary for continual growth in the Lord. However, the dark revival I was experiencing was similar but in the most polar opposite kind of wicked way. There were new doors opening for me daily, not in a good way, and I was weaker than ever. I still hadn't told a soul about the illegal transactions I was engaging in; only my crazy cousin really knew the truth. Everything seemingly looked good from the outside. My wife's baby bump was now very noticeable; our local church was growing like crazy, which I had a hard time rationalizing because I was their pastor.

Everyone would have taken a quick glimpse at my life and would say, "You are totally blessed, and I was. I guess that is part of the problem. Everyone is so busy with their schedules that it is hard sometimes to take much more than a quick glance in someone's direction to even notice they are headed for destruction. I was so lonely and felt so fake—outwardly smiling and trying to help people, preaching every week—but inwardly, I was screaming for someone to notice and intervene by attempting to stop the madness.

Another door was opening, another opportunity for my depravity to manifest itself through the horrible choices I would make, yet another battle to face. My life was actually like a locomotive getting ready to derail while heading through a small compact town square. The damage would be significant, and when it happened, everyone just wouldn't be able to help themselves. They would have to watch the drama play out at every foot of the train wreck as it comes crashing to a screeching halt after demolishing building after building.

It was getting close to Christmas, and the house was perfectly adorned with multiple trees, beautiful lush garland around the fireplace and on the door facings, and shining lights that put off that soft glow like only they can. I love Christmas for the beauty of its true meaning and the food, but my wife had a totally different love for Christmas. She was moving a little slower this year and needed more rest as she tackled decorating one room after the other during her last trimester of pregnancy. She was meticulously detailed with her Christmas-decorating pursuits every year. It was basically like we were moving every November.

The day after Thanksgiving was the day everyone in the family knew packing began. I was half inebriated from a turkey hangover this year, but I just popped another pill and got the totes out of the attic. It wasn't just a Christmas tree and some illuminated candles in the window sill for her. Nope, that would be much too basic, and she took it to a whole new level. She'd often say, "C'mon, Scroogie-woogie, it's the birth of Jesus. This is not just any holiday we're celebrating, right?" We had Christmas dishes, cups, and glasses. We even had a Christmas toothbrush holder. Yep, I'm not kidding, y'all. Every time you would pull our toothbrush out of Santa's sled, the music would play to the lyrics of "Santa Clause Is Coming to Town." I would always allow it to cause me more shame every morning and evening while I was brushing my teeth because it would repeat these lyrics, "He's making a list and checking it twice, gonna find out who's naughty or nice."

I felt judged by a Santa Clause toothbrush holder because I would totally be on the naughty list for Christmas, only coal in my stocking this year—well, besides the tie I always received. That's what you buy, preachers, apparently. I secretly wanted to smash Santa in his sled with my fist, like a meteorite falling from the sky, while laughing maniacally but could never bring myself to follow through with it. Would it feel good? Yes, most definitely. However, it would just tick Mrs. Clause off, and I was obviously married to her. She loved it, and I probably hated it as much as she loved it, so I kept my complaints to myself because I loved her with all my heart. It was one of the only *Santa* decorations in the house. We didn't do the whole Santa thing because we were conservative Christians. Why would we let the jolly fat man in the red suit steal Jesus's thunder, especially on His birthday? Nope, not this year, Satan! Whoops, I meant Santa.

Christmastime not only comes with decorations but it also comes with plenty of stress and financial strains. We had to blow a wad of cash to get our almost three-year-old some plastic toys that he would only play with for ten minutes on this magical day. Couldn't we just regift the same toys from last year? It would probably work. We will end up donating them to the Good Will anyways in a couple of years, right?

"Why are you stressing so much about the money this year?" my wife asked.

You already know why. I had $700 to come up with this month. I had managed thus far to take the checks to the bank from my preaching engagements and deposit a little but keep some cash out of them to buy my pills. The church had us on a modest salary at the time, which helped to pay our bills; and we lived in a parsonage, which was a house the church owned that was provided for the pastor as part of his benefits package. I knew the extra money would be harder to track, and I had made it work so far. However, most churches don't schedule conferences or additional meetings during this time of year, so I didn't have any way of earning extra income.

What was I going to do? I couldn't risk getting caught, but I didn't want another unwelcome visit from those withdrawal symptoms.

I remember having a conversation with some of the guys from the church about how cool the new flat-screen televisions were. We talked about a Monday Night Football fellowship meeting for the men's ministry with some nachos and chicken wings at the parsonage. All we needed was a big flat screen. Normally, the church folks would scrape us up a little Christmas offering, which was always a blessing. However, I just knew the guys were gonna come through for me this year and get me a fifty-five-inch flat-screen TV. I had heard some talk about it through the grapevine. To my surprise, they superseded my expectations by gifting me a sixty-five-inch brand-new flat-screen TV that just came out. It was bigger and better. Whoa! Merry Christmas to me! What surprised me also was the timing. They brought it to me early because by the time Christmas was over, we would only have a little more than a month of football season left. To them, it was more than just a gift to me but a gift for all the guys to enjoy.

The only thing that could stifle my Christmas joy was the phone call I received from my wife while she was on her way back home from the grocery store. She had a minivan that we bought used, with too many miles, that was just a piece of junk. I hated it, but she just had to have it to meet the need of our growing family, according to her. Well, the motor blew and left her stranded on the side of the parkway with her bulging belly while wearing her Santa hat. I hopped in the car and headed that way while calling a mechanic, who was part of our church family, to see if he could go get her van with his tow truck. He agreed and met us there on the side of the road. I transferred all the groceries to the trunk of my car while the semis sped past us, almost blowing us out of the emergency lane. He loaded the minivan up, and we followed him to the exit. We were less than five miles from our house when my wife said, "I think I just peed on myself, or my water might have broke."

What! Not today! Well, I guess it would be today. We don't always get to schedule these things. She was very close to her due date, but she went over with our last little guy, so this was quite a surprise. I whipped the car around and headed back down the parkway at a dangerously high rate of speed. We made it to the hospital successfully, and about five hours later, our second baby boy was born. All those same mixed emotions overwhelmed me again as I felt sorry for this little guy because he had such a screwed-up dad. I made sure my wife was resting well before I went back home to gather the things we would need for our brief hospital stay before bringing our new bundle of joy home. She gave me a list with all the specifics because during this busy season of life, we didn't have the bag packed for the hospital just yet.

I ran by my parents' house to check on my other little guy. He was having the time of his life with his papaw and mamaw. Daddy looked so weak, and it was hard to see him this way. The chemo and radiation were taking its toll on him physically. Cancer is just a big bully that I would love to punch in the face for the whole of the human race. I would put up the fight of my life, and it wouldn't be a fair fight either. I would claw, bite, scratch, and give it everything I had in me. It had already taken my grandparents on both sides and was now whipping my once barrel-chested daddy with the vein-filled Popeye forearms. He didn't even look like the same guy, but spending time with my oldest son always brought a smile to his face. He said he reminded him of me when I was his age so much.

Both of them spoiled him rotten, and I was convinced that they would have literally killed me for some of the things they would encourage him to do and then laugh about it. My old man had an ornery streak in him, and he would try to teach my son cusswords, which he always referred to as "lil wordy dirts" that seemed like they were just a normal part of most country folks' vocabulary in our area. He would do this because he thought it was cute, in his opinion, but the main motivation was to embarrass me. It worked on multiple different occasions, especially at the church house. Goodness! Way to go, Dad. Hopefully, he wouldn't repeat the same process with the newborn.

By the time I made it back to the house, I made a beeline to the cabinet because I had been on almost twenty-four hours without a pain pill, and the addiction seemed like a school of piranhas gnawing away at my soul. I opened the lid on my pill bottle and immediately put an Oxy through my lips, onto my tongue, chomping on it like

I used to chew up a Flintstones vitamin when I was just a little boy. The pill bottle didn't make the same rattling sound as it used to, so I nervously poured the rest of them out in my hand and began to count them like a pharmacist. No! No! No! This couldn't be happening again. How could I have possibly mismanaged my prescription? I should still have a few.

I went to my other secret location, which was located in my in-home study, and pulled the big Bible concordance off the shelf. My other orange bottle was tucked away securely, but it didn't have the pills I thought it would. My surplus was running even shorter at this point, and it was probably due to the multiple trips up and down the steps to the attic to get the Christmas decorations, which caused my joints to feel like they were going to explode. This can't be real. I'm going to be short, right before Christmas, which would be the same time we would be bringing the baby back home from the hospital. I couldn't be going through withdrawals at this time. What in the world was I going to do?

I just sat down in the middle of the floor, miserably desperate, feeling sorry for myself, but praying for a solution to this major dilemma I was facing. I needed a sling and a stone, just like David, to slay this Goliath in my life. I could reach out to Daddy to see if he would let me have a couple of his pills, but even if he complied, it still wouldn't be enough. By this time, I was lying on the floor in a fetal position, looking at that awesome sixty-five inch flat-screen TV that was still in the box. The guys were supposed to come over and help me hang it above the gas fireplace in the living room, but the excitement from the baby coming so suddenly postponed the installation. It would be a couple of weeks before my hillbilly hero would get his prescription filled, and I would run the risk of getting caught by my wife, especially during this time of year when money was usually so tight.

My cell phone started ringing. I answered it while lying on the floor. It was my mechanic buddy who picked up my wife's van.

He said, "Well, I hate to call you so close to Christmas with bad news, but it will need a new motor, and my cost will be three thousand dollars."

He assured me that he wouldn't charge me a dime for the towing or the labor, so I gave him the go-ahead to order the motor even though it would totally drain our little savings account. The stakes just got much higher, and now I was in a pickle. I could sell a few guns that I had collected, but who would have the extra money this close to Christmas to buy them from me? How was I going to solve this equation without getting busted?

I called my cousin to inquire if she knew anyone else who might be willing to get rid of some unused medication. She said she just received a call from a friend who had recently had a death in their family and left all their prescriptions behind. When she called her name, I knew exactly who she was because I preached at her funeral service. She had suffered through chronic pain for years and had a massive heart attack, killing her instantly a week before her eightieth birthday. Her son, a corrupt sheriff's deputy, actually reached out to my cousin to see if she wanted to buy them for $10 per pill. I told you, my crazy cousin had connections, and she would be able to help me once again. Praise the Lord! Well, I know He really didn't have anything to do with it. God is Holy. How could He still use such an unholy vessel like me?

I had tracked down some pills, so the first part of this equation was solved. Now the tougher part of the problem was figuring out how I was going to pay for them. As I got up slowly from the floor, my eyes went back to that brand-new television that was so conveniently sitting by the door, still in the box. The war in my mind began, and just as you suspect, I was getting ready to lose another battle as the justification protocol kicked in again like a famous defense attorney in my mind. The church members bought this for me, so if I sell it, it's really no different than stealing money from the church. I would never do that, would I? What kind of story could I cook up to tell the guys about the flat screen?

My mind was going in a hundred different directions, and it seemed like the room was spinning around me. How could I ever live with myself? This was so wrong! What would I tell my wife? I didn't just go through all these random but logical questions one time. Oh no, they repeated continually the whole way back to town as I borrowed my daddy's truck to return the TV to the local Walmart because the sixty-five inch flat screen wouldn't fit in my Camry. I had schemed up an awesome plan in my mind, and I was convinced that it would work. I would tell my wife that I stored the TV at my parents' house because we wouldn't be able to hang it safely over the fireplace. We would need to build a frame or reinforce the studs so it wouldn't fall off and hit one or both of the boys, taking a chance of seriously injuring them. It wouldn't make total sense to her, but she shouldn't question it, hopefully.

The trustees at the church would need to meet with the financial committee to get approval to do this because it was the church's house. She, of all people, would understand how long it could take to get the ball rolling on this as it bounced between the different committees and then went to the church members for final approval in a monthly business meeting, which couldn't be scheduled until after the first of the year. This was the only time in my ministry that church polity and the bylaws worked out in my favor. I hated all that political stuff, which seemed to cause more problems than solve them. Oh well, this scheme would definitely buy me some much-needed time, so I voted yes to it secretly. What would I tell the guys who actually orchestrated the purchase of this awesome gift? I got it! "My wife is suffering from postpartum depression. You know, the baby blues." They would totally believe it too.

Some of those same fellas went through this with their wives because I remember vividly counseling them through it. It wouldn't be appropriate to plan a Monday Night Football bash while she was trying to overcome postpartum depression. They would never even realize that the TV had never been installed. If they asked, I'd tell them I stored it at my parents', or better yet, I didn't want to install the television without them. I was holding out to watch the first game with them. Well, what do you think? I know I'm a horrible manipulative liar. Hear me out, please, before you judge me once again.

I had already scheduled two big conferences in January. I was planning to use the offerings I received from those preaching engagements to buy another flat screen and get it installed before the guys or my wife found out. I would purchase the same brand and model, and no one would ever know. This was just a temporary solution because I needed some quick cash, and I needed it now. It was the best plan I could think of to keep me from going through withdrawals. I didn't want my wife to think I had fallen sick again with another stomach virus the week of Christmas and leave her with the responsibility of caring for a newborn by herself while she was trying to recover from the soreness of delivery. I had to do what I had to do, so I called the church treasurer and asked him to leave the receipt for the television in my office because I would need the purchase information to fill out the warranty information from Samsung. He believed me. He never suspected that I had concocted another plan for the flat screen. He let me know that he couldn't wait for the buffalo dip at the first men's football fellowship. What he didn't know wouldn't hurt him.

I returned the flat screen and walked out with the cash in my hand—flawless victory or so it seemed to be. I headed straight to my cousin's house with plenty of cash in hand. The TV was more expensive than I expected, so I could get my Oxy and probably pay for half of the new motor for the minivan. It's all working out. I was doing everything I could possibly think of to continue to feed my secret addiction. I brought my wife and newborn son home on a Friday evening. So many people from our church showed up to surprise us. There was enough food to feed an army. What a blessed homecoming! Those older purple-haired ladies were passing the baby around like a hot potato, and my other little fella was entertaining a group of older men. They just loved his feisty and spunky little personality. Hopefully, he wasn't repeating the bad language he heard and was taught by his papaw. We were so blessed! I had plenty of pills, my wife and baby are both healthy and home in time for Christmas, and there are probably more than five different pies sitting on the kitchen counter. It couldn't get much better than this, for sure.

I thought we might get some rest, but the baby wasn't having it that night. I let my wife rest and took the night shift walking the floors and singing every hymn I could think of, trying to get him settled down. He wasn't a hymn guy just yet, but he surprisingly liked my version of "Ain't No Sunshine" by Bill Withers until I made it to the part with the thirty-seven I-knows. There were probably not that many, but it seemed like it when you're listening to it. I would just skip that part while singing the opening verse over and over. This song was more like a prophecy of things to come.

The next morning, my wife woke me from my sleep, and she was in full-blown rage mode. I had no idea what was going on and had never seen her so worked up before. I tried to calm her down by reminding her that she had just delivered a baby and needed to think of her health when she showed me the search history from my laptop. Unfortunately, OxyContin wasn't my only secret addiction even though I don't really think I was addicted to porn then. You couldn't have convinced my wife that I wasn't at the time. It wasn't like I was watching it every day. My interest was piqued in it by something that was mentioned in one of my counseling sessions with a young man from our church, so I foolishly looked it up.

There was really no excuse for it. She couldn't be physically intimate with me during the last month of her pregnancy, and I justified turning to this perversion as an alternative. It was by a satanic conspiracy that it all happened. I had been meeting with a guy who had been visiting us to counsel him during his failing marriage when he confessed his porn addiction to me. Sometimes, in the process of trying to help someone through a tough time, you can get exposed to their darkness. I'm not blaming him for what my heart selected my eyes to look at. It was totally my fault.

She told me it was no different than committing adultery in her eyes even though I didn't quite see it that way. I was reminded of what the Bible said repeatedly by her like she was the preacher instead of me. She said, "You know lust leads you to commit adultery in your heart." Jesus did say that, not exactly those words, but she knew what it meant. She called me a pervert. I had never looked at myself that way or anyone who looked at porn for that matter. Maybe she was right. All I know is that this was going to be the most difficult and stressful Christmas in my life.

I agreed to start counseling with a pastor in another town to help with fixing what was broken in me to salvage our marriage, according to her. The stress of all this coming at me at once was more than I could bear, and my Oxy cravings multiplied tremendously. I wasn't worried about divorce because it was something neither of us believed in. We took our wedding vows seriously—well, maybe she took them to heart more than I did—but I really wanted our marriage to be great. It broke my heart that I broke her heart and that she couldn't look at me the same. I wanted to earn her trust back more than anything in the world, but it seemed like the damage I had done was beyond compare. I couldn't even trust myself. I was a ticking time bomb just waiting to explode and injure those around me, who I cared about the most from the shrapnel. I had no idea that counseling would open the door to more secrets—some of the darkest ones in my life.

Chapter 6

The Exploitation of Innocence

The next day, I called a counselor, who was a ministry acquaintance of mine and a man, who I knew could help me. While I was on the phone with him, sitting in my church office, a few of the men I had placed in leadership came in with rather long faces. I thought for sure my wife had called them even though that seemed out of character for her. I assumed she made an exception in this case, and they were getting ready to ask me to resign.

One of them said, "May I shut the door?"

I gave him permission to grant us some privacy for this surprise meeting that was just sprung on me out of nowhere. I was thinking about the severity and potential lifelong implications I would have to deal with at the conclusion of this off-the-record conversation. Most issues in the church that become big issues hardly ever start as big issues at all. They are normally just selfish ambitions that collide with personality conflicts, which create division and lead to tribalism. I call it church drama. It's real and sometimes ugly, but whatever it was, I was really not in the best mindset to handle it with biblical discretion at this particular moment.

One of the men, who I assumed was elected as the spokesman for the group, said he had a serious question that he needed to ask me. Another fella, who I had known for more than twenty years, interrupted him as nicely as he possibly could and began to express the church's and the community's love and adoration for me. He assured me that they weren't there to accuse me of anything but needed some information to head off some swirling rumors. By now, I realized that I was in more trouble than just on the home front. My time at that church had probably come to its bitter conclusion.

"Did you take the flat screen back to Walmart to pay for the repairs on your wife's minivan?" the gentleman asked.

What? This serious meeting was really about the television and not my marital problems or my secret addictions. I was so shocked that I had been caught but so relieved that I hadn't been exposed for the darker things I was also guilty of committing that I almost fell out of my chair. I wanted to tell them the truth and just end it all because I was beyond weary of all these secrets and needed help. However, when I opened my mouth to respond, all I heard was, "Yes, brothers, I was just too embarrassed to let anyone know that we were in a financial jam."

They all encouraged me to reach out to them, so they could help if I was ever in a similar situation financially. They also informed me of how I got caught. Apparently, a teenager, of a family who had been visiting the church, witnessed me return the flat screen and mentioned it to someone who mentioned it to someone else, and it finally got back to the guys at the church. That's how it always happens in a small town, right? Word spreads fast.

On Christmas Eve, those same guys drove my wife's minivan back to the house and handed me an invoice that said, "Paid in full! Go get your TV back. We are ready for some football!" They totally covered the expense of the three-thousand-dollar motor. I was so thankful but so ashamed. That night was the first time I ever actually thought about killing myself, and once that thought entered my mind, I couldn't seem to shake it no matter how hard I tried. Christmas was weird, and my wife would barely speak to me. She heard about the whole surprise meeting over the television fiasco but still didn't know the whole truth. She asked me what I did with the rest of the money from the flat screen. When I was hesitant to answer her, she thought I had spent the money on porn sites and even suggested I might be visiting the red light district in a bigger city about an hour and a half away.

Finally, something I wasn't actually guilty of. I told her I had never spent money on porn or prostitutes. My answer didn't seem to make her feel any better. She asked me if I was ever even attracted to her before she started having babies. She felt less than beautiful because of the pornography she discovered on my laptop. She also told me she visited a lawyer to research her options for a divorce. I was shocked because I didn't think I would ever hear the D-word come out of her mouth. Maybe she was just trying to scare me or maybe she was giving me the warning I deserved. Either way, we had some dark days ahead of us, and I honestly couldn't see the light at the end of this tunnel. I told her that I loved her, that she was the most beautiful woman in the world, and that I was willing to go the extra mile to prove it to her and eventually earn her trust and respect once again. She raised her head, and her face changed from a disgusted look to a fearful look as she asked me to come clean about everything.

She said, "If this is going to work, we can't have any secrets going forward. I need you to come clean now because I can't have a relapse again in six months if something else comes out."

I thought, *What do I have to lose? I'm going for it.*

Our marriage is already falling apart anyways so I told her my darkest secret—the one that has hurt me the most and left thick scar tissue on my mind. You think I told her about the OxyContin, didn't you? Believe it or not, it was something else. I had a secret I had been carrying with me for years that I hadn't shared with anyone up until this point. I opened up and let it rip. It felt so good to finally share it, but it was way too much for her to handle, considering what she had already endured with me. So I kept the addiction issues to myself for the time being even though I really wanted to confess everything. I could tell that she'd had enough when she put her hand up, like a crossing guard directing traffic, and said, "Stop! I can't process this right now."

I get it because it was a lot to process, and she didn't have any medication like I did to take the edge off things. You see, I wasn't introduced to porn by the young man I was counseling. His demons just reopened a familiar door and led me through the dark revival of another old habit I thought I had put to death.

My wife had no idea what I experienced in my early teenage years, which started all the way back in seventh grade. It seemed like I was a pro at keeping secrets because I learned how to perfect that art at an early age and had never mentioned this to her or anyone else for that matter, not even one single time. It was my secret. I'm coming clean with it now publicly for the first time.

When I was thirteen years old, I was introduced to pornography by the most unlikely person. She was my favorite teacher throughout my middle school days. We started as just friends, and she became my safe haven during my seventh-grade year because I was the new kid in school. And her room became my necessary refuge. I became popular once the other students got to know me and all the girls liked me because I wasn't shy like the other boys. She got to know my parents and started out treating me like a nephew. She was like the aunt I never really had. I would go everywhere with her and her son, who was just a few years younger than me. If they were going somewhere after school or over the weekend, I went with them. She bought me anything I asked for and treated me like one of her own children. I had no idea that her relationship with her husband was rocky, to put it lightly.

I didn't realize it at the time, but I became her refuge too. But she didn't look at me quite like a nephew, a son, or treat me like the rest of her students. I remember the first time she shared her feelings with me. She told me that we were gonna get married one day. It was shocking but also flattering. How could an attractive, educated, and successful woman be interested in a kid who struggled with pre-Algebra? I had come to find out that she was more than just interested but became infatuated with me, especially after her divorce was finalized.

We started hanging out even more without her son. She would take me to her house, and no one would be there but just the two of us. I never really connected the dots, and neither did my parents, somehow. They just trusted her. We would go to the movies and out to eat all the time. It was like dating before I was allowed to date or even had my driver's license. I was just a thirteen-year-old kid, who loved playing video games and listening to my Sony Walkman with the latest rap and country music cassette tapes. I had a diverse pallet when it came to music.

On the other hand, I didn't have a diverse pallet when it came to porn. It actually grossed me out. I couldn't imagine that people actually did those disgusting things to one another. I remember the excitement in her voice when she told me she had a special movie for us to watch. It was an old VHS tape of some porn from the eighties or appeared to be a little dated. It was just like any other movie night at her house, with plenty of snacks and soda to drink.

When it finally got to a sex scene after about ten minutes into the film, she picked up the remote, which was lying between us, scooted in close to me, and began to rub on my inner thigh. Looking back on it, she was ready to exploit my innocence after losing any innocence that remained from the graphic scene. I remember moving past the shock and awe of it as she coached me through different scenes we witnessed together. It was like she was a play-by-play analyst, except this wasn't a football or basketball game we were watching.

She asked inquisitively if anything was appealing to me. I really didn't see anything appealing about any of it. It actually looked painful and unwholesome. I also felt uncomfortable about the way she looked at me while the movie was playing. When she looked into my eyes, it was much different than the way she had ever looked at me before. As a kid, I could never remember anybody looking at me like that before, with such a strong lustful desire. Her voice had also changed as she leaned in and, with a seductive whisper, asked me, "Is there anything in the film that looks like fun to you, because we can do that together?"

She asked me point-blank, "Is there anything you would want me to do to you, right now?

When I declined, she was never forceful, but you could tell it disappointed her. She had certain expectations and specific goals for exposing me to these pornographic films, but her plan backfired. I hadn't fully gone through puberty yet. I barely had any peach fuzz under my arms. My sex drive didn't exist at this time. I didn't even know what a sex drive was. I really didn't think too much about girls in a sexual way until after she educated me that night for my first porn class.

Later, she asked me if I thought she was attractive or even sexy at all. She so desperately wanted me to desire her. The first person I had impure thoughts about after I had been sexualized wasn't her. It was a girl my age, who happened to be a beautiful blonde-haired, blue-eyed cheerleader at my school. The impurest of those thoughts were wondering what it would be like to kiss her or hold her hand. I remember sharing this with my teacher one evening while we were on our way to a movie, and I could tell that it hurt her. It wasn't intentional on my behalf. I was being honest. I'm sure my unwilling-ness to engage wasn't helping her self-confidence or her self-worth, and I can remember feeling really bad for her. She told me these were just natural things people do with each other when they cared for each other deeply.

She would say, "I know you care for me, so why don't you want to experience these things with me?"

I told her I was scared, and I was. I just couldn't make myself believe that all the people I knew did these things with each other. It didn't appear to be very loving, but then again, what does a thirteen-year-old middle-school student know about love?

One night, we were just playing around, wrestling, and chasing each other through the house when I tackled her on the bed. She escaped from my grip and got up to turn the lights off, and then the wrestling match continued in the dark. That was the first time I ever desired her for some reason. Thankfully, her son was actually home that night and walked in on us. He was probably in fifth grade at the time, but he could tell that something was inappropriate about it. It was awkward because you could sense her excitement because I was beginning to desire her, but it was mixed with frustration because we were hindered before things could escalate. Who knows what would have happened if he hadn't come into the room?

I shared much more with my counselor, so I will spare you all the crazy details. But one thing that I can tell you, it ignited a lust-ful passion in me for pornography. I battled this perversion through middle and high school sometimes on a daily basis. It gave me the wrong view of girls and women. God designed sex to be enjoyed between a husband and his wife. It was a beautiful gift given from the heart of God to married couples, but I never grasped that perspective until I started reading the Bible.

After the Lord saved me, I willingly forgave this woman even though she made a negative impact on the hard drive in my mind and opened some dangerous doors that gave me a skewed perspective on what love actually looked like. However, I really believed that she deeply cared about me at the time, and I knew I could count on her to help me with anything if I ever needed her. I never looked at her as a pedophile or a predator until after I had children of my own. It gave me a totally different perspective.

By that time, I had already forgiven her, so it didn't matter. And I didn't want to revisit those old skeletons in the closet of my past. I also never really viewed myself as a victim. I was her victim as she groomed me to have an adult relationship with her when I was only a child, but I never really considered myself through the whole relationship. I just felt bad for letting someone down who had done so much for me. It was really confusing for a seventh grader to process all these things, but I also had some guilt associated with it later as I grew older and looked back on it.

Once I turned sixteen years old, I could've put the brakes on it but chose not to. It was a transactional relationship, and I used her for my own personal selfish benefit. She was a very generous lady, especially when it came to me. She bought the first set of aftermarket rims I put on my sports car when I turned sixteen. She was always buying me nice things and giving me money. I really didn't want a romantic relationship with her, but I was on testosterone overload at the time. I also didn't want the fountain of financial blessings shut off. She is still alive but much older now, and we are actually Facebook friends. I know it's weird, to put it mildly. I see her from time to time at the grocery store or in a restaurant, and we always speak cordially to one another. She actually still calls my elderly mother just to check on her and to chitchat from time to time, and they have a friendly relationship. She ended up remarrying a good man and wanted me to perform the wedding ceremony, but it was just a little too weird for me.

I have never thought about reporting her but have often wondered if I was her only romantic student crush. Could there be others just like me who were also exploited or even worse? It was something that haunted me for some time when my wife and I started having our own children. I realized how this would negatively affect my wife now that she knew about the sexual trauma from my past. She just continued to turn more and more away from me. I tried to tighten my grip, but it was evident that I was losing her.

Chapter 7

Coming Clean

It was time for my first counseling session. I absolutely dreaded it with every fiber of my being even though I got acquainted with the guy who agreed to counsel me a few years ago. He was the guest speaker for one of our conferences at church and did an amazing job. This made it more awkward for me, for sure. He had been in ministry twice as long as me, and I trusted him. My wife also trusted him, which was even more important to me. He was a jovial little fella with a big heart and a soft voice.

I knew he would shoot me straight and hold me accountable. I also knew he would stay tight-lipped about the pornography and keep things totally confidential. I wasn't even going to mention the medication abuse. He wasn't a licensed therapist, but he had been through some obstacles personally and in his ministry and could definitely point me in the right direction. I made sure I had plenty of medication, but my stomach was in knots. I really didn't want to go through with this, but it was priority number one for my wife, so I agreed.

It's kinda like agreeing to a root canal, a colonoscopy, or a prostate exam, in my opinion. They may be necessary, but it's not something that you ever look forward to. No dude has ever said these words: "I am so jacked up about my prostate exam. This will be an awesome experience and the best day ever! Whoa Yeah!" It just isn't going to happen. Men aren't wired up like that by divine design. At least, this guy cared enough about me to readjust his whole schedule to meet with me. He also played football and loves mixed martial arts (MMA) and something called jiujitsu, which is kinda like wrestling with choke holds and joint locks. I don't know much about it, but he did.

I remember him telling me about how he got bit by the jiujitsu bug one night as we were all eating at a local restaurant after a service. I assumed it was some kind of insect, maybe like a mosquito, until I figured out it was a popular martial art in Brazil. I think he moved his family to Brazil to do some "kingdom work," as he called it, for a couple of years and studied it while he lived there.

We should have some things in common, and it would probably go much better than I anticipated. Granny always said, "What overwhelms you today will bore you tomorrow." It would probably be just a few sessions anyways, which would be enough to convince my wife that I am invested in our marriage and willing to put in the work to get it back on track. That's the ultimate goal through all this. I couldn't lose her!

I pulled up in the parking lot and reluctantly got out of the car. He greeted me at the door and was very hospitable. He had just used a French press to make us some coffee, and it was amazing. He didn't dress like normal pastors who were normally adorned in khakis, a button-down shirt, and a sports coat, especially in the ministry circles I was affiliated with. He had on jeans with an untucked Columbia fishing shirt, a flat bill cap covering his bald head, and was wearing some Hey Dudes. I told him I would've brought my fishing pole if I had only known we were going fishing. He laughed while saying, "Life is too short and ministry is too tough for all that religious garb." I gave him a hearty, amen.

We made some small talk about life, hobbies, and ministry over coffee; and then he asked me to lead us in prayer. I was very comfortable with him and prayed the most spiritual prayer ever. I even included some "thees and thous" in there just to make it sound official. As soon as I concluded my oration with "In Jesus's Name"—of course—he asked me a question that rocked me to the core. It was a serious question that caught me off guard, like being struck with a lightning bolt. I didn't really know how to answer him. He just cut right to the chase and didn't really give me time to work my way into the session like I thought he would.

The counseling sessions I had conducted in the past didn't seem to move so quickly. It's like he just saw right through me. He told me to take a minute to process it, and then he asked me the same question again: "So when did you fall out of love with Jesus, to the point you quit trusting Him?"

I really didn't feel like he was judging me. He smiled at me and said, "I know you probably didn't think I was gonna hit you with a haymaker from the opening bell did you?"

He assured me that my healing would be contingent on my love, trust, and obedience to Jesus. I had to get to the place where I could be content with Him even if I lost everything, including my wife. Was Jesus really enough for me? No! I wanted to convince myself that he was, but my addiction controlled me. All my wants, desires, and dreams were wrapped up in a pill bottle. I was guilty of loving my wife, my kids, the ministry, and even my Oxy more than the one who willingly gave his life for me. I felt more dirty than I ever did before and knew that I couldn't really come clean about my addiction.

We talked about the "pitfalls of pornography"—I believe that's how he said it, if I remember correctly. He talked on and on about the importance of accountability. He told me to give the laptop to my wife or get rid of it and to disable the internet on my phone and in our home. He obviously didn't think I was responsible enough to make good decisions right now, and he was correct in his assessment.

He kept saying, "Don't give place to the devil in your weakness. Go back to the cross and fall in love with Jesus again. Close your eyes and look at him hanging there, bloody and beaten, all for you. He is right there waiting on you with His arms spread wide."

He asked me if I believed there was more forgiveness in Jesus than sin in me. I nodded affirmatively but didn't really think He would want to forgive someone like me and offer me another chance. He also thought me and my family needed a change of scenery, so he instructed me to take a sabbatical from preaching for a month to invest in what he called the "big two," or the two most important relationships in life, which he described as the relationship with the savior and the relationship with your spouse. He said the first relationship would be key in healing the second relationship. I told him that a sabbatical would be next to impossible for me. The church couldn't make it without me. He laughed and said, "You just admitted to me that your heart isn't really in it and that you have been merely going through the motions for quite some time now, correct? So really the church is already making it without you!"

His final instructions were: "Schedule a vacation, find childcare, and go invest in the big two, okay." He prayed for me and prayed over me, and then he hugged me like he would never see me again and watched me walk out the door. I was mentally exhausted trying to process the questions that penetrated my heart like a spiritual arrow. I was also somewhat frustrated because I realized I was a habitual liar to everyone, including myself.

Outwardly, I appeared to love Jesus and was actively engaged in ministry, but it wasn't for Him. My mouth would state my love for Jesus, but my heart was far from Him. What a mess! I got back home and told my wife what he recommended, and she began to cry. I thought to myself, *Good gravy, I can't do anything without making her cry.* Now, she cries when I talk to her.

She said, "He's right! We both need to work on the "big two! We have a business meeting coming up, so why don't you talk to the men at church and see if the church could grant you a leave of absence?"

I immediately told her what a bad idea I thought that would be. She said, "I can't believe you're not gonna take his advice. It's like going to the doctor, receiving the proper diagnosis, but not taking your medicine."

That seemed to strike a familiar nerve with me. Don't you know the definition of *insanity*? It's doing the same thing over and over and expecting different results. We have hit a wall, and we need to let the church know. You can call a men's meeting or I'm gonna get on the phone and tell them everything. I can't take much more of this! We are not just going to go to a counselor and nod our heads, going through the motions, during the sessions to never apply or follow through with what he instructs us to do. Wait a minute! Was she in the room, like a fly on the wall? That was exactly the plan in my mind. If this guy tells me to stand on my head and bark like a dog, should I comply with that too?

I called for the men's meeting at 6:30 p.m. this coming Friday. As I walked into the church sanctuary, it almost felt like a tribunal to me. I took the floor at 6:30 p.m. sharp and called the meeting to order like a parliamentarian and asked one of the oldest gentlemen in the front row to open the meeting in prayer. Once he finished, I let the guys know that I was suffering from ministry burnout and needed a break. I told them this would be beneficial in my plans for the longevity of ministry with them and explained it would only be for a month.

I was as committed as I ever was to the church, but my wife's extended postpartum depression had taken its toll on me and my family. They seemed to understand, and I promised to schedule non-monotone guest speakers while I was on sabbatical, which only made them feel more comfortable about me vacating the pulpit for a month. A zealous young know-it-all with a sharp tongue and a critical spirit, who had just moved in from another state and united with our church, took the floor and informed us that a pastor is much more than just someone who preaches sermons but the God-ordained leader of a local church.

How could we possibly go forward with a part-time pastor? Well, this didn't sit well with some of the guys, and several of them began to give their opinion at the same time. And I interrupted to maintain order in the meeting. He made a valid point but in the wrong spirit and with the wrong attitude, according to some of the men. He had the right position but the wrong disposition and immediately lost the respect of the men in the room. A wise older gentleman stood to his feet and began to address the men. He was a respected member of this church and a very godly man—one of those fellas who rarely said much, but when he did, it was on point.

He reminded them of my years of service and also of the words of our Lord, which was to esteem others higher than ourselves.

He said, "Brethren, instead of piddle-farting around in this meeting, we should pray about it and bring it up at the church business meeting for a vote this Sunday evening."

I agreed and entertained a motion to adjourn the men's meeting and got one immediately. We dismissed in prayer, and everyone exited the sanctuary somberly. I didn't have a good feeling about this upcoming business meeting. I have already told you about the little things turning into big things in southern rural churches. To top it off, I already disliked business meetings, especially when one of the items of business would be pertaining to me personally. I mean, if the church didn't vote to approve my much-needed break, what could they really do? I guess they would hold me hostage against the advice of my counselor. I guess we would find out soon because the meeting was on Sunday evening.

I told my wife about the conclusion we had reached at the men's meeting. She already had our bags packed and had scheduled childcare for our eldest son, who had just turned three years old. My parents would be more than happy to watch him, so Daddy could teach him some more cusswords. The baby was growing but still needed his mother to eat, so we decided to take him with us. We figured we would head out to Pigeon Forge, Tennessee, for the first part of the week, and then try to reserve a beachfront condo in North Myrtle Beach and stay the rest of the week.

Saturday was a peaceful day, and I was convinced it was just the calm before the impending storm coming at the business meeting. Sunday morning service went great! The building was packed, and we had several first-time visitors. I preached about Joshua facing the overwhelming obstacle of his Jericho and how the Lord intervened. We almost broke the attendance record of 205, which was achieved at last year's Sunday morning Easter service. We had a pancake breakfast, which some of our older members thought was a form of bribery. You feed them pancakes today, and it will take a filet mignon to keep them coming back, as some were saying. I guess that's what Jesus thought after feeding the five thousand with just five barley loves and two small fishes. He moved on from that to center-cut steaks with Sister Schubert's yeast rolls. However, 199 in attendance was great for us without the enticement of the pancakes. It seemed like there was a month of Sundays between those two services partly because my nervousness wouldn't permit me to take my normal Sunday nap in between the services.

Finally, the time had arrived. I stepped up on the platform, braced myself securely behind the bulky oak pulpit, and called the church to order for our regularly scheduled monthly business meeting. The crowd appeared to be a little larger than normal even though business meetings were exclusive to members of the church. There were people present that night I could never remember attending a business meeting as long as I had served as the pastor of this church. This did not help me with my nervousness at all, it just escalated it. All the reports were read and approved, and all the committees reported. There was a committee for everything. We had a committee called the recommendation committee, whose sole responsibility was to make recommendations for what committees were needed and who should serve on them. Good gravy! This side of church government was always utter ridiculousness to me.

It was time to open the floor for new items of business, and I did so. As soon as the last word came out of my mouth, Mr. Know-It-All sprang to his feet. He informed the church about what we discussed at the men's meeting on Friday night but never put my leave of absence in the form of a motion.

He said, "Church, before we address this in this meeting, I have a question for our pastor that I would like to hear him explain publicly, and I know you do too. Pastor, please explain to us why you took your Christmas gift, which consisted of sixty-five inch flat screen television back to Walmart to receive a full cash refund."

He said it like I was on trial, and he was cross-examining me as the prosecuting attorney. You could tell people were shocked and somewhat confused by the expression on their faces. I didn't really know how he knew, but nothing surprised me at this point. The church realized—well, at least the older members did—that he did not follow the rules of parliamentary procedure because there was not a live motion with a proper second. So the floor wasn't open for discussion. I didn't correct him or ask him to take his seat because it would have just made me look even more guilty.

The mechanic, who fixed the minivan, spoke up in my defense. He said, "He took the flat screen back for a refund to cover the expense of the motor I put in his wife's minivan. He had every intention of buying another one after the first of the year and didn't say anything to the church because he was embarrassed. Everyone knows how hard money is to come by around Christmastime. Some of the guys found out about it and scraped the money together to pay for the expense of the motor in full after they had a private meeting with him."

When he finished his speech, I just couldn't take it anymore. I was at the breaking point, and the dam of my internal emotions came crumbling down under the pressure of stress and anxiety I was under. I began to weep uncontrollably while standing behind the pulpit in front of everyone. Once I got my emotions under control and could actually form a sentence, I told the truth, the whole truth, and nothing but the truth. It was so freeing! Do you remember the story about the buffalo and the cows? Well, sometimes when you're at your breaking point even cowardly cows do brave buffalo stuff.

If you think they were shocked over the television, they hadn't heard anything yet. I asked my wife to leave because it just wasn't right telling her right along with everyone else. She needed to be out of the spotlight, so she loaded up the children and went home. It was the most tense, awkward moment in the history of this rural congregation and it would all be recorded by the church secretary.

I looked over at the mechanic and publicly thanked him for standing up for me. I really appreciated it, but it wasn't the truth. I could tell lie after lie but just couldn't stand the thought of this good ole boy defending a lie that I told.

I spilled the beans by saying, "Church, you deserve to know the truth, and I am going to tell you the truth. But the truth is going to hurt you, and that is not my intention. I never wanted to find myself in this situation under these circumstances, but here we are. The truth is, I'm an addict. After the motorcycle accident, I developed a dependency on prescription pain pills and didn't have the self-control to take them the way they were prescribed to me. The more I took, the more I needed to take. I even started buying them secretly, and that's what I used the money from the TV for. Please forgive me! I need help!

"My wife had no idea, and I was requesting the sabbatical because our marriage is in shambles all because of me. She is not going through postpartum depression any more than I am. If there is any depression in her life, it has been brought on by my selfishness. I have been looking at pornographic websites, and she discovered it on my computer. I have been seeing a counselor, and he says I need to take some time off to work on my relationship with Jesus and my wife."

You could've heard a pin drop. Everyone just looked at me with amazement, except the folks who were so disappointed that they couldn't stand to look at me at all. No one gathered around me for prayer. No one said anything. I had to escape this moment, or my heart was going to beat out of my chest. I did the only thing I could think of and just walked down the middle aisle, right between everyone, got in my car, and drove home. This was the beginning of the end for me.

When I arrived home, my wife was lying in the bed in the fetal position, just waiting to hear of our fate. She asked if I resigned. I probably should've, but it actually never crossed my mind, or I would've made that announcement also. I told her that I lied to her before when she asked me to come clean, but I wasn't ready, but I was ready to tell her everything now. She never even rolled over to face me. I sat down on the edge of the bed while still in my suit and tie and told her everything. I had never seen anyone cry that deeply in my life. I just couldn't take any more shame and guilt and really couldn't imagine hurting her more.

She muttered three words through her snobs and unbridled weeping. No, they weren't "I love you!" That would be wishful thinking on my part, right? She said, "Please just leave!" I didn't say a word as I picked up my suitcase, which was already packed and sitting on the floor, next to the bedroom door. I grabbed my Oxy and locked the door behind me before I left. Where was I going? I could go to my parents, but then I would have to explain what was going on to them, which would be the third time in one evening.

I was exhausted, so I drove to the nearest town, which was the same town the motorcycle accident occurred in. I was sitting at the same intersection, waiting on a red light to change to green, just watching the cars drive by. And it was so surreal. It was like I relived it all, every bit of it, over again, in a flash while waiting on the green light. I was so paralyzed by fear; I couldn't press the accelerator with my right foot. Cars honked at me and swerved out around me, trying to make it through the intersection before the green light expired. So much transpired in such a short time, it had only been a few years. If only I had the power to go back and change it all, I would in a heartbeat. It felt like I was in the twilight zone. Where was I going to get a motel? I could've rented a room in our little town but really didn't want to add bed bugs to the list of things I was currently fighting.

The motels would be better in the bigger town, so the drive was worth it. I decided on a Hampton Inn and crashed there for the night. Tomorrow would be a new day, but would it be a different day? It probably wouldn't compare to the pain and the sweet release I experienced on this day. I had so many bittersweet, mixed emotions that I couldn't get my mind to quit racing long enough to fall asleep. What would the rest of my screwed-up life look like, and would it even be worth living? Would it just be a continuation of staggering through the darkness? Thoughts of suicide plagued my mind now more than ever. I needed help!

Chapter 8

New Beginnings with Old Demons

I finally fell asleep as the sun was rising after watching multiple episodes of a show called *Dexter*, which is about a cold-blooded serial killer who only preyed on the individuals who caught an unfair break from the justice system. He just couldn't tolerate the injustice and would take matters into his own hands by dismembering his victims and disposing of their corpses. He worked in forensics and lived this insanely messy double life, where he had to continuously sneak around and habitually lie to keep from getting caught.

I had never seen a show that portrayed a serial killer as the hero, but it was more than interesting to me. I even thought of myself as the Dexter of pastors while watching the show. I never thought of killing anyone besides myself, but I felt this strangely bizarre connection to him. My cell phone awoke me from sleep, but I missed the call because I couldn't seem to locate it underneath all the pillows and the covers on the bed. It started ringing again, and when I saw the number, I realized it was my mother. My wife had spilled the beans on me, undoubtedly.

When I answered the call, I expected to hear a barrage of negativity coming at me like the bullets from a .50 caliber machine gun. However, when I heard her frantically screaming my name, I realized something was terribly wrong. By the time I made it to the hospital, Daddy was already on the ventilator with tubes, lines, and hoses running all over his body. My poor little momma was hysterical.

According to her, he just passed out and hit his head on the floor. She tried for a few minutes to resuscitate him but wasn't successful in any of her attempts. By the time the EMS made it out to their residence, which was located in the middle of nowhere, he was already turning that pale blueish color. The team of doctors came into the room and gave us a bleak prognosis after running multiple tests throughout the night. The golf ball–sized tumor was growing rapidly, and the radiation wasn't working. The mass grew to the size of a softball in a little more than six months and totally shut off his airway. He was just too weak to risk the surgery.

They also informed us that his cancer had spread to his brain. I stayed in the hospital with him the whole week. Where else was I going to go? I wasn't welcome at home anymore, I guess. I called my wife many times, but she hadn't returned any of my calls at this point. I was sitting there, in that hospital room, with my old man, thinking how I wish I could switch places with him. I deserved this much more than he did. He served his country, loved his wife, and raised his children.

The beeping from all the machines was almost deafening, and the ventilator kept repeating this sound that reminded me of a horn on a clown's car from one of the shows I used to enjoy as a kid. It's almost like I could hear the evil laughter of Satan himself every time that machine would beep, like my life was nothing more than a big joke—just an evil game I got caught up in the middle of somehow. I felt hopeless, helpless, and totally out of control as my life seemed to be set on fire, and I couldn't do anything to prevent it from totally burning to the ground.

I thought back to what my counselor said to me. It was like he was in the room talking with me. His words were like gold retrieved from a memory vault by the Holy Spirit. Sometimes, things take a little time before they become impactful. Sometimes words, statements, phrases, or even biblical principles don't hit us directly between the eyes right when they are spoken, but they will in God's perfect timing. He recalls them so they may have a powerful effect on us at the right time and during the right season. I could see him sitting there behind his desk, leaning back in his chair with his hands clasped firmly behind his head while saying, "The mind is the battlefield for spiritual warfare, but the prize is the heart. Don't just surrender your heart without a fight to anyone but King Jesus. Keep your eyes on him in this battle and trust Jesus and the power of His Word to change your stinking thinking. Renew your mind!"

I guess we try to blame everything on the devil, right? It has been human nature to blame shift ever since the garden of Eden. In Genesis chapter 3, Adam blamed Eve and Eve blamed Satan, who tempted her while in the form of the serpent.

My counselor said sternly, "Quit giving Satan more credit than he deserves. He is a defeated foe, but you are giving him some of the same attributes as God. Can't you see that? You talk about him like he's more powerful than he really is. He is not omniscient [all-knowing] or omnipresent [limitless—everywhere at the same time].

"I know you don't really believe that he is, but who cares what you believe if it doesn't change your actions and your attitude? Your doctrine can be a gun barrel straight on every biblical subject. But unless it changes your heart, your mind, and your life, then what good has it accomplished other than informing you on what to do, right? The devil didn't make you do any of this. He is nothing more than a terrorist, who encourages you to believe lies about yourself. He realizes that you are the imago Dei, an image bearer of Jehovah, so he assigns unclean spirits to attack you constantly.

"Don't you realize that he believes there is a special purpose for you to accomplish? He believes it more than you do from hearing you talk the last thirty minutes or so. You think he's taken you hostage and convinced you there's no way out of this unfortunate hostage situation. Demons have whispered the same old lie in your ears a thousand times, brainwashing you to believe God won't pay the ransom to get you out of this terrible situation when Jesus already paid the ransom more than two thousand years ago on the cross. It is finished! The war has been won! Satan is a liar, bro!

"The only one holding you hostage and keeping you from experiencing victory is you. We make choices and don't realize that we are choosing the consequences of those choices until we begin to reap what we have sown, but then it's too late to take it back, and we can't wish it away. The only thing better than being set free from the bondage of sin is actually believing it and living in kingdom authority. When did you quit believing that the gospel was powerful enough, not only to save you but to set you free from any form of bondage?

"Listen, bro, either Jesus is alive and we have hope or He is dead and we're all doomed and headed for destruction. Why are you living like He's dead? If you really believe He's alive then ask yourself this question. No, on second thought, write it down."

He searched through his desk drawer for an index card and a Sharpie marker and slid them across the desk to me when he found them while saying, "Write this down: 'Jesus is alive! What will I face in this life that is more powerful than His resurrection?'"

I paused and looked up patiently at him, waiting for the answer, but he informed me that only I could answer that question for myself. The correct answer is, nothing! Nothing is more powerful than the resurrection of Jesus, but I really didn't believe it because my life said otherwise.

My life said, "Porn is more powerful than His resurrection! Addiction is more powerful than his resurrection! Satan is more powerful than His resurrection! Temptation is more powerful than His resurrection! All of my lies and manipulations are more powerful than His resurrection. My self-defeated mind and emotional collapse were more powerful than His resurrection."

I fell to my knees and ended up totally prostrate on my belly, with my forehead pressed against the cold tile on the hospital floor, while crying out to God to forgive me. I felt like I'd been totally saturated with an outpouring of His grace and washed squeaky clean. It was painful and liberating at the same time, if that makes sense? God did exactly what I asked him to do. He graciously forgave me, but it wasn't a magic spell that would fix all my problems. But at that moment, I really didn't care about anything else but getting right with God.

Jesus became so much more to me than just a spiritual genie while lying on that hospital floor. I realized at that moment of desperation that I had been treating Jesus just like my Oxy bottle. I only opened the lid when I needed my fix. I was more in love with medication than I was with my master. I was more in love with porn than my provider. God truly forgave me, but being forgiven and walking in forgiveness are two different things. How could I ever possibly forgive myself?

My wife came through the door of the hospital room in the ICU unit and embraced me. We were both weeping, praying, and confessing our faults to each other as I apologized to her over and over again. When we finally came back to the reality of our broken lives from that moment of embrace, we had a host of nurses giving us the stink eye. I went back home that night and slept in my bed. This was not the sabbatical my counselor suggested, but I had come clean with everyone, including God, and was instantaneously different. I could tell it, and my wife could see it in me also. It was a conversion after my conversion. Sounds kinda weird, huh? The conversion of a Christian pastor. I confessed Jesus was my savior as a eighteen-year-old teenager and was baptized in a deep hole in Fishing Creek, but I had never felt God as closely as I experienced him in that hospital room.

The next day, we made one of the toughest decisions in my life. Mom and I decided to turn off the ventilator based on the doctor's recommendation and commit Daddy to the hands of our Great Physician. Our family gathered around him to say our goodbyes and told old stories while we laughed, cried, and prayed. He lasted a little less than an hour as he took his final breath. I drove Momma back to the house. And when we walked through the door, she headed straight to the gun safe and said, "Here ya go, take all these guns outta here. You know we have some rough people in our extended family, who might try to break into our place to steal these now that they know he's gone."

There it was! That Beretta 9 mm was my favorite gun, just like the one Martin Riggs carried in the movie *Lethal Weapon,* which just so happened to be one of Daddy's favorite movies. I loved shooting that pistol when I was younger, and so many wonderful memories flooded my mind when Momma handed it to me. I hadn't shot it in a long time or even laid eyes on it for a long time.

After the funeral, my wife and I decided to take Momma to Pigeon Forge over the weekend. Things were still awkward between me and my wife, but she was giving me another chance, and I was truly grateful for it. One of the deacons at our church told me that he called a local preacher to cover the pulpit for me this coming Sunday. I told him about my plans to head out of state with my family over the weekend, and he agreed it would be a good idea. He said he would take care of everything while I was gone and made me promise him I would get some rest. He slipped three folded and extra crisp one hundred dollar bills into my pocket before he walked away. What a blessing! We all had a good time—well, as good as we could have, considering everything that had just transpired in our lives.

My wife still hadn't said a word to my mother about my recently and publicly confessed sins. She knew her heart was already broken over the passing of my daddy and didn't want to hurt her more with the news of my shenanigans. I know I'm partial to her, but my wife is probably the best Christian I have ever met.

Just when things felt somewhat normal again, my cell phone rang. It was my mechanic friend from the church, who called to give me the breaking news from the business meeting. I thought to myself, *What business meeting?* I had no idea really what was happening, but he seemed to be very upset. My head was such a mess that I didn't even realize it was Sunday.

"Some of the deacons called a special business meeting, and the church voted you out as pastor. They are only gonna give you two weeks to move out of the parsonage," he said, frantically.

The leadership I set up—the very men I poured myself into to enrich their lives—didn't even bother to call me. We just had a business meeting last Sunday evening—one they will never forget, I'm absolutely certain. They called a meeting without me, behind my back, to give me the boot. Surprisingly, I wasn't even upset. I was more numb by everything that had transpired. I told my wife, and it was a setback that hurt her deeply. She blamed me, of course, and should have. It was definitely all my fault, and I didn't handle any of it the way I should have. Well, I just buried my old man, lost my ministry, and would be expected to move in just two weeks in the worst part of winter with a wife who didn't trust me.

It all just seemed like a never-ending nightmare and horrible timing. We drove back home that evening, and I wondered what the next chapter of my life would look like without the ministry. Serving as a pastor was more than just a calling to me, and God continued to use me even in my darkest hours. I always wondered why. Why would he use someone so messed up? But the truth is, we are all messed up in just different ways. We are beggars, simply pointing other beggars in the direction of the soup line. We are all kinda like busted *piñatas* without any candy inside. We can't really offer God anything but our hearts.

I believed in our utter sinfulness and preached it, but I believed it more now than ever before. We cannot attempt to live the Christian life through the power of our intellect or own physical strength. It takes God's strength, my friends! My goal over the next two weeks would be to get a new job, find a house to rent, and move everything while doing my best to keep my wife from leaving me. I know, it seems a little overwhelming. I assure you, it was. This is all so crazy, no one would even believe me if I told them.

The only solution I could think of was for us to move in with my momma and rent a storage unit we really couldn't afford to store our furniture in until we rented a house. Who needs two weeks to move? Not this guy! I had our stuff packed up and delivered securely to a storage unit by the following Sunday, I think I accomplished this feat so quickly just to prove a point. It only made things tougher on my family, but that seemed to be my spiritual gift—making things more difficult.

On a positive note, the local bank was impressed enough with my resume that I got a call for an interview. I had banked with them for years and knew most, if not all of, the employees. The move caused my already aching joints, knees, and back much more stress, and my pain got to an intolerable level. I needed more pills and couldn't risk running out. I also couldn't risk my wife catching me purchasing more pills illegally. She was watching me like a hawk sitting on a power line, scanning every field for the next meal. Foolish decisions win foolish prizes, right? I didn't want to win any more foolish prizes.

I prayed and prayed for Jesus to stop my cravings. Prayer never really seemed to work for me like it did for other people. But to my surprise, I noticed a difference, and I was thankful for it. However, not enough of a difference to stop me from revisiting that cabinet to look for my daddy's pills, just like I did during my teenage years. It was like a déjà vu moment where I found myself back in the same house standing at the same cabinet for the same reasons. Déjà vu is really weird, but it wasn't this neurological phenomenon that I was experiencing at all. It was just me, still fighting the same old demons on the same old battlefield. I had fought this battle over and over, for years, ever since high school; and I was still staggering through the darkness.

Chapter 9

More than I Can Handle

For the majority of my life, I've heard well-meaning folks say, "You know the good Lord will never put more on you than you can handle." Here's the problem with that statement: I have never come to that conclusion from reading the Bible. I don't think Joseph, who went from the pit to the prison to the palace, would agree with this statement either.

The apostle Paul would strongly disagree also. He was beaten, pelted with rocks, whipped worse than a horse on more than one occasion, shipwrecked, incarcerated, bitten by a snake, and betrayed. Jesus died on a cruel, rugged cross after being almost beaten to death by the providence of God. Sometimes, we come up with these so-called biblical principles that aren't anywhere to be found in the scriptures.

Our personal experiences aren't equal to or will ever be emphasized higher than scripture. My personal experiences would also confirm that this statement couldn't be true because I was coming to the end of my rope. The bank interview went great, but they never called me back. When I reached out to them to see if they had filled the position, the gentleman said, "We really wanted to hire you, but some folks came into the lobby from the church and told us some things that you supposedly said and did, but we don't believe them. You're too good of a preacher and a blessing to our community to get involved in the things they accused you of, but we just didn't want some big account holders from the church to move their business elsewhere.

"God will open a door for you, you know that. He is faithful! I hear they are hiring over at the new factory. Maybe you should try it there. You know, brother, the good Lord will never put more on you than you can handle. Praying for you and your momma! Tell her I said hello."

The blessings of living in a small town outweigh the cursings, but when you are a public figure and the center of negative attention, it feels more like a curse. Everywhere I went I could see people huddle up to gossip. I eventually got used to the whispers, but my wife just couldn't handle all the stress and anxiety from the swirling rumors surrounding our family. It was the same old story spun in a new way, and it would finally make its way back around to us.

We were quickly running out of money and started maxing out credit card after credit card. Thankfully, we had good credit because we didn't have any savings. My addiction depleted our savings more than a year ago. I was keeping us afloat by selling my guns here and there, and I even sold some of my old man's guns but not the Beretta 9 mm. I wouldn't part with that one even though it wasn't worth $350 because of all the good memories I had made with my daddy shooting it on the farm.

A couple of months later, my wife seemed nauseous while fixing breakfast. She gagged a couple of times while scrambling some eggs for me and the kids, so I took over the cooking duty and suggested she lie down. I heard her crying in the bedroom of the house we claimed as our own—the house where I was reared. It was my old room, and I couldn't believe I was living in it once again. I scraped the eggs out of the pan quickly and went to check on her. She said, "I think I'm pregnant again." Sure enough, after not one but two EPT tests, we realized we would be the proud recipients of baby number three.

After going to the doctor, she was farther along than we expected. She was so thankful but didn't feel quite ready to bring another child into this world without a house of our own or a steady income from dependable jobs. This process repeated itself for five more years with two more babies, giving us a total of five children—each born roughly two years apart, give or take a couple of months here and there.

I was promoted to a supervisor position during that time at the factory the guy at the bank recommended to me. We had saved up some money but was still living with Momma in my old room. She loved the children being in the house and for getting the opportunity to spoil another baby every couple of years. I was miserable and felt stuck in the rut of working ten-hour days, just to come home for a couple of hours, and then go to bed only to repeat the whole process over again. I felt like I was in prison.

Our plan was to move to another place and try to start a church, a much different church than I was just voted out of—a church where loving people in their sin mattered more than anything else, a church where people just didn't talk about healing, deliverance, redemption, and freedom but walked in it every day in victory. A real family who maintained a spiritual and emotional hospital where Jesus the Great Physician was more important than dress codes, Bible translations, monthly business meetings, and cultural traditions—so much more than a building but a living, loving, and laboring community that lived life together through the dark and dreary valleys and the highest mountain peaks of success.

Please know that the only thing I had ever desired more than OxyContin was to preach, pastor, and lead disciples into a different life than I was experiencing. God rekindled my passion for ministry that night on the floor of that ICU unit while I was lying at the foot of Daddy's bed. He was getting ready to die, and I was getting ready to come alive, and I didn't even know it. Jesus is always on time but not my time. I had so much passion just burning on the inside of me but was only given a few opportunities to preach since that night made me somewhat infamous in our little town. If I received a call from a church, it was always somewhere out of state or where people didn't know the scoop on me.

The crazy thing that hurt me the most wasn't the decision to have a private meeting without me, or the fact that they voted me out, or them giving me just two weeks to move in the dead of winter. Rather, it was them totally writing me off. I really needed community more now than ever, but no one seemed to care or wanted others to find out they were still associating with me, I guess. No one, not a single person from that church, ever checked on me or bothered to pick up the phone to see if we had food. They were good to me and my family because I served there for many years, but when I needed them the most, in the darkest time of my life, they totally ignored me like I was dead. I would see them out in public, and they wouldn't even look at me. My family and I became invisible to them while I staggered through the darkness.

I guess the relationships I thought I had with friends, who felt like family to me, were at worst totally fake and at best trans-action-based. They paid me to preach and build the church, and I performed to the best of my ability, which wasn't good enough. I turned into their professional preacher. When I confessed my sins, that terminated the invisible contract I suppose. I realize I was guilty of hurting them, and I actually hated myself for it because I truly cared deeply for these people. I hadn't looked at porn in more than five years and didn't even have the desire to anymore.

My experience with overcoming pornography, through the power of the resurrected Christ, gave me several opportunities to help guys at the factory. I wasn't preaching in a pulpit at the time, but I was still called to full-time ministry and just wanted to help whoever I could. I was gonna try to make the rest of my life count because nothing was more powerful than His resurrection. I was still fighting the war on the battlefield in my mind with my addiction. I had good days and bad days. There are always highs and lows in whatever season you are going through in life. Hopefully, God would give me the strength to overcome OxyContin too.

My wife was taking care of babies and had an experienced tag-team partner in my momma to help her every day. She also was overly cautious in helping me manage my pain pills by keeping me accountable every month like a hybrid CPA mixed with a pharmacist. Our marriage wasn't perfect by any means, but we were committed to Christ and each other. I had so much to share, so much to invest from the multitude of battles I had just survived, but I felt like the best years of my life were passing me by. I'm sure Moses felt like that out on the backside of the Midian desert for forty years before he ever had his burning bush experience. God didn't forget about him and had a purpose for him to walk in. I was hopeful the same would be true for me.

Even though I was voted out of the church as the pastor, my wife and I knew the importance of investing in a local church, and both of us felt the Lord directing us to attend the church our counselor was leading in another town. He planted this church years ago and had been serving as the lead pastor from day one. It was a good drive, but it was worth it because it helped me and my wife to heal through so much trauma. I wasn't expected to lead or preach. At first, I felt useless just sitting there, but I didn't realize God was picking up the broken pieces in my life and putting me back together one piece at a time.

I remember the day we went to see him to ask him if we could attend his church. He said, "It's not my church, it's the Lord's church. And if you aren't welcome here because you're not perfect and have made some mistakes, I guess I'm not welcome either because I have missed the mark of perfection also."

They welcomed us like family, didn't push us to serve, and loved my family continually. He really pulled me close and invested in me like no one ever has in my ministry even though I never really felt like I was worth the time he spent with me. He believed in me when I didn't believe in myself and would speak blessings over me continually.

He would always say, "Remember, God is gonna use you and has already factored your stupidity and the mistakes you will make into the equation before He ever called you, so you don't have the power to mess it up. You're walking to your purpose, but soon you will be walking in your purpose." I wanted to believe him so badly, and I wanted God to use me so desperately.

About two years after attending church with him and getting plugged in through serving in that community, he called me and said, "Let's grab lunch." When we sat down, he asked how long it had been since I came to his office all those years ago, and I said a little more than seven years ago. He asked if I thought restoration could take that long.

I said, "I have no idea, but I want to lead a congregation again so much. It's almost all I think about."

He said, "Well, there's an opportunity for you. Are you ready?"

My first reply was, "What about my past?"

He let me know that he filled them in on it without giving all the scandalous details while laughing jovially as he did often. He was only serious when it came to helping people and preaching. The rest of the time, he was joking and laughing or laughing and joking.

He said, "I told them you had been walking in the Spirit for more than seven years, which was longer than the great tribulation period will last according to the book of Revelation, and God had fully restored you."

He then leaned over like he wanted to tell me a secret, and when I leaned toward him, he whispered, "The past is only alive in your mind. Move on! God can take the rest of your life and make it the best of your life. He can take your mess and turn it into a message with a little time."

They were excited to meet me and wanted me to preach to them next Sunday. Wow! I was blown away. Was this too good to be true? Was I dreaming? God was going to potentially use me in pastoral ministry again, and I couldn't have been more thrilled.

I fell in love with the people from the first time we visited with them, and I preached there every Sunday for a couple of months before they elected me as their pastor. The church had seen more glorious days in the past, but that was before their pastor had a scandalous affair with one of the deacons' wife. It was about an hour and a half drive one way, and they were a small congregation without much money. They agreed to pay for my gas, and I kept my job at the factory and drove back and forth for two years before we bought a house and moved less than a mile from the church property.

God blessed us by multiplying the church weekly. During the third year, I quit my job at the factory and was back in full-time ministry. God is faithful! He brought me full circle and restored my ministry. On Easter Sunday morning, we had more than three hundred people in attendance in that small building, which was busting at the seams. What a service! It seemed like we picked up momentum from there and kept seeing the gospel transform lives as more and more people came. King Jesus was saving souls, restoring marriages, and using this church to make disciples in this town. God was drawing individuals who were battling all kinds of addictions to our church, and this was exactly what I had been praying for. I wanted people to live differently than me and not have to go through the same hard knocks and rough patches I had to experience.

Yes, I was still pushing through the pain, but I hadn't taken OxyContin in a long time because the FDA banned it. I had the same doctor all these years later, but he was prescribing me a different pain medication, which is called Hydrocodone. I still had to take four pills a day, as needed for pain, and my wife still held me accountable, as well as a few men with similar backgrounds from our church family. This was when the religious people began to come out of the woodwork. This church wasn't as strict and staunchly religious as the last church, but there were still some of those folks in the congregation, who stuck together like a swarm of hornets.

I started hearing things like, "Our church is changing so much. We don't even know all these new people. Some of them have tattoos and don't dress very modestly. We saw a lady kneel at the altar last Sunday morning in a pair of shorts. She mooned the whole congregation, and you didn't even say a word about it, preacher. All the new kids are so loud and distracting that we can't even hear the sermon. Hasn't anyone ever taught them to show respect for the house of the Lord?"

"Oh, by the way, speaking of the sermon, we notice that you have been using some different Bible translations as you reference verses. We have always used the *King James Version*, so why are you using something different? We can't even follow along with you. Are you trying to be trendy? I like the suit and tie much better than the jeans and pullover you have been wearing. I can't worship to these newer songs. They're awful! Don't think you are getting rid of the organ, it was donated by my granny."

The scribes and pharisees who Jesus encountered were obviously still alive and coming to the church I was ministering at. I love them! You have to because they get on your nerves and cause so much trouble when you don't put a definitive check mark in their preferential boxes. They are even good at trying to play the Holy Spirit in the lives of younger converts by telling them how they should dress and what genre of music they should listen to. You know, because some of that stuff that has lyrics about Jesus sounds worldly, just like a rock band. Why are so many older church folk so closed-minded and impatient with younger Christians, who are just trying to figure out church lingo and what to expect? Why do we elevate our personal preferences even above Bible doctrine in some cases?

I had an older lady in the church who probably thought she owned it because her granddad and her dad were both deacons who served the church years ago—you know, back in the good old days, which she referred to all the time. I wonder if they were really as good as she remembered them being. Anyways, she met me out in the foyer as angry as she could be while I was standing with a whole family of brand-new converts, Christ had just gloriously saved. All of them had just been baptized at the conclusion of the Sunday morning service. They still had wet heads and were getting some encouraging congratulations as people from the church family hugged their necks and shook their hands as they exited through the front double doors of the building.

She was so angry because she didn't think I baptized them correctly, so she commenced to tell us about it. She snobbishly said, "Preacher, they were facing the wrong way when you took them under the water!"

I looked rather confused at her, which didn't help to improve her already negative attitude. She continued, "I've been a member of this church all my life and I have never seen anyone baptized facing the wrong side of the church. What are we going to do about this?"

I said, "What do you mean by the wrong side of the church? Are you talking about the direction they were facing when I baptized them?

She shook her head in agreement while saying, "Yes, that's exactly what I mean. Did I stutter? I mean what I say and I say what I mean, don't you?"

I asked her this question, "Do you think the pastors who have performed the baptisms here in the past were probably right-handed?"

She replied, "I don't know, and what kind of question is that, and why would it matter?"

I said, "Well, I'm left-handed, ma'am. I turned them facing the other direction for the purpose of getting my left arm, which is my strong arm on the middle of their back to make it easier to baptize them."

I guess my simple explanation wasn't good enough for her because she protested a little longer and finally walked out. Those poor folks, who had just publicly declared their faith in Jesus, had their excitement stifled by a grouchy old religious woman, who just wanted to fuss loudly about something the Bible is silent on. We have no doctrinal instruction about what hand to use when baptizing someone or if they should be facing the east versus the west, okay. I'm sure one hand is as good as the other one, and the direction is unimportant. Why can't we be loud where the Bible is loud and just keep our mouths shut where the Bible is silent?

I was still excited about this second chance opportunity and wasn't going to let a few peripheral issues sidetrack me. I was convinced 2020 was going to be the biggest year of ministry for me yet. We announced our theme on "Vision Sunday," which was the first big Sunday service after the new year; and we were ready to *go, grow,* and *glow* for our Lord. What could a church with twenty-twenty vision accomplish? It was a little basic and maybe even corny, but we come out of the gate on fire to start the year. But something happened in mid-March of that year that we didn't see coming, and we're not ready for—Covid-19.

I had definitely never led a church through a global pandemic and didn't know anyone else who had experience with something like this either. It was definitely an unprecedented time we were trying to navigate through and proved to be the toughest ministry hurdle I had ever encountered. Nobody really knew what to do. Our church went from a place of refuge to a political battleground. There were so many different opinions that I couldn't even process them all. The local, national, and world news was covering the pandemic around the clock. It was nonstop info bombarding us, and none of it really made any sense to me.

People were getting the coronavirus and were dying! Our leaders at the church were scared and began to panic. We were continually having meetings through different platforms that many of our older folks could not figure out how to get to work. We had entered a time of mass confusion, and we desperately needed to figure out how we were going to continue to fulfill the pending task of the Great Commission. We were shut up in our homes and placed on lockdown. I know so many churches that suffered through the pandemic to such a degree that many of them will never recover. I wanted to continue to have in-person services only on Sunday mornings while attempting to practice social distancing, but the idea quickly came under scrutiny.

With the changing opinions and growing concerns, it would be impossible to please everyone as the leader of the church. I was caught between a rock and a hard place and spent the next year, just like most other ministry leaders, utilizing social media as my only tool to stay connected to a world paralyzed in fear and wanting nothing more than to disconnect physically. I became the pastor who cared more about having church services than keeping our church members safe from the virus to some of the church members because I wanted to have one in-person service per week. I had already experienced a quarantine, so to speak, because my wife and I stayed in the house most of the time to keep from facing people in the town we recently moved from.

She couldn't take the negative attention and the dark spotlight shining on her because of me. I knew this wouldn't be good for our church, but what could I do? My hands seemed to be tied. I went through a very dark bout of depression, to say the least. I was confined to my home once again just a few years after God began to bless my ministry. It just didn't seem right. I was just so frustrated!

As I would share my frustration, some dear old saint would always remind me, "No matter what you go through, the good Lord won't put more on you than you can handle." I can only imagine the look of disdain on my face as this wanna-be spiritual phrase continued to be repeated to me by just about everyone. What I was getting ready to go through next seemed to be the very last straw that would break the camel's back. I will never forget the day my wife came crashing angrily through the spare bedroom door, which we had converted into a studio to shoot some videos for our church family. This place was my safe haven, and I immersed myself in creating ministry content to keep everyone encouraged.

I was in the middle of recording a message from our *Jesus Is Better than Anything* series from the book of Hebrews when she screamed, "You're still at it! I knew I couldn't trust you! You're such a liar!"

I was so thankful I wasn't in the middle of a live stream on Facebook. It would have set the new record for the most views, I'm sure. She was as irate as I had ever seen her, and I immediately began to inquire what in the world was going on to cause her belligerence while I was giving her the deer in headlights look.

She screamed, "Don't act all innocent! You are the pornography preacher. Yep, that's what you are! You get up and brag about God's power to deliver people from the bondage of their addictions while you secretly enjoy your lustful desires. You are the biggest addict in our church and the biggest hypocrite I've ever seen. You are worse than Judas who betrayed Christ."

She hurled the laptop at me, and I almost fumbled it, dropping it on the floor. She didn't ask me to leave this time because she had already planned her escape. I couldn't catch up to her with my barely functioning knees, hips, and back. She got in her minivan and was gone. My heart was racing, and my head was spinning. I just lay down in the front yard because I felt like I was going to pass out. I had been guilty of telling lie after lie for years, but God really transformed me that night on the floor of the hospital room. I was telling the truth! I hadn't looked at porn since that miraculous experience with Jesus that totally redefined my life. My world finally came crashing down all around me, and I was actually innocent this time. I thought maybe, just maybe, this was lingering punishment that had been building up for years, like the heat in a pressure cooker that blew up all at once. I guess I'm finally reaping all the wickedness I have sown.

As I was trying to process the events in my mind, I just felt this smoldering rage that continued to level up in its intensity. I prayed so specifically for God to intervene while I was just lying there in the yard. I finally picked myself up after crawling halfway to the house. I located the laptop, which she threw at me like a fundamental, two-handed, overhead basketball pass, to shockingly discover what my wife was so upset about. It was porn and a whole lot of it, but who searched for it? All of a sudden, my heart was in my throat as I nervously walked to my eldest son's room. He was a musically talented teenager by this time, who aspired to be a worship leader one day. He did not like sports but had more musical giftedness in his little finger than I had in my whole body. I was praying so loudly in my heart that it was just spilling out of my mouth as I knocked on his door and entered his room.

Everything felt like it was in slow motion. He was lying there, all snuggled up in the thick comforter on his bed, sleeping like a baby. He should still be a baby. Where has the time gone? My mind went back to so many different, beautiful memories of him growing up. It was like a mental photo album that took me from his birth, through his childhood, to this present moment as I sat there in his desk chair watching him sleep. I gently patted him on his foot, which was the only thing slightly exposed from underneath his bedding. He sat up and greeted me with that big grin he's always had. That grin could light up the darkest room. It was almost like looking at a carbon copy of myself.

I said, "Little buddy, I hate to hit you with this right out the gate first thing in the morning, but we need to have a serious conversation. I know you have been using my laptop to access your online classrooms. Is that the only thing you have used it for?"

He replied, "Sure, Dad! What's going on?"

I told him about the showdown during lockdown between me and his mother, which was rather hard to believe that he just slept through. I figured the neighbors could hear her screaming. He dropped his head and confessed as big tears ran down his cheeks and dripped off his chin.

"I am so ashamed of myself. I didn't mean for it to get this bad," he said as his voice was breaking.

I was so hurt that I felt like I had let him down. It was my job to protect him as his dad, and I blew it. I think the thing that stung the most was when I realized my lust and desires had been passed down to him. We spend our whole life protecting our children from danger and from the things they are fearful of. I did a good job thus far, I hoped, but I couldn't keep from thinking who was going to protect them from me. Was I the worst enemy?

I know I should've punished him, but I just couldn't bring myself to do it. No electronics, television, or video games for the rest of his life was what I was thinking, but it just didn't seem like punishment enough for such a dark and dangerous sin. Would it make me an even bigger hypocrite if I punished him? Why would I punish him when he was already repentant and remorseful? But at that moment, I came to the awesome realization of how God must have felt watching me stagger through the darkness all those years. My son had tiptoed in and out of it, and my heart was broken for him. I didn't want to beat him down; I wanted to hug him and love him more during this tough moment in his life.

Oh, the overwhelming grace and love of God that had been so lavishly bestowed on me. We sing songs about His grace being greater than our vilest sin, but for the first time, it just clicked. The light bulb came on about his marvelous grace, and I was just basking in it. Oh, how He loves us so! Let me say, I believe it's both biblical and loving to discipline your children; but at that moment, I was paralyzed by the sweetness of His grace, so we both just sat there crying. I was ashamed that I had let my savior and my son down, but I was also so thankful for grace and forgiveness that I couldn't even express it through words. God didn't condone my sin or my son's sin, but he wasn't excited to drop His Thor-like gavel in judgment to condemn us; he was lovingly dealing with me paternally instead of judicially. Hopefully, the Lord understood my tears in that moment of reflection. I believe he did.

After a few minutes, I told him to take it all to Jesus—everything! There's nothing more powerful than His resurrection. He's the only one who would forgive him, cleanse him, and give him the power to overcome this lustful temptation. I shared some of my personal struggles with him when dealing with the same thing. We prayed together, and I walked out the door, hurting but hopeful and thankful for the presence of the Lord. Sometimes, God will allow things to creep into our lives that we can't handle, so we are forced to look to Him as our only solution. It's in those times we see his power, are reminded of His grace, are covered with His love like a warm blanket, and ultimately grow closer to Him.

Oftentimes, God uses trials, tribulations, and obstacles to knock off the rough edges and conform us more to the image of Christ. This is a necessary part of our growth. God would never tempt us to sin, but he can use sinful seasons as teaching tools to help us grow. God is not the author of sin and tragedy, which occurs naturally as the result of the fall of humanity in the garden of Eden. It's been messy since that fatal day. God will allow you to go through more than you can handle, but He will never give you more than He can handle. Ahh, I like that statement much better. I'm thankful for His presence and His power.

Chapter 10

Believe in Miracles

I don't know if you believe in miracles or not, but I certainly do because I was getting ready to witness one of them in epic proportions. After the talk with my son, I tried reaching out to my wife on her cell without any success. I drove over to her parents' house and saw her van parked around the back. I was assuming she was attempting to hide it from me. I repeatedly knocked on the door, but no one ever answered. I drove to multiple places to find her, but it was like she had vanished.

The city we lived in was like a ghost town from the effects of the pandemic. It was so strange to drive by the mall and see the parking lot empty. Everyone had buttoned down the hatches and took cover in fear. That evening, my wife pulled into the driveway to get some of her personal belongings so she could go stay with her parents. She told me she had to drive for more than two hours one-way to find a lawyer's office that was actually open so she could file for divorce. Oh, wow! I didn't think I would ever hear her say those words. I told her to cancel it because I was innocent. I talked to our eldest son after she went berserk, and he confessed to looking at the pornography on my computer.

She said, "How low can you possibly go? Is there any line you won't cross? Any length you won't go to try to cover for yourself? There's no way I would ever believe that our boy would look at something like that because he is not a freak or a pervert like you."

I said, "Just ask him! He'll tell you the truth."

She replied, "The only thing he will tell me is what you told him to tell me. I can't believe you would force or bribe our son to lie and try to cover for your sorry hind end. I told you the next time would be the last time. I will fight you to take everything, including the kids. It's over!"

She didn't even get a bag to put some of her stuff in. She just gathered it all up in her arms hurriedly, told all the kids to get in the van, and slammed the door on the way out. I thought I had earned some of her trust back but figured out that she didn't trust me at all and probably hadn't for years. My ministry was over. and I was all alone—in the prison of our house. My family would be broken apart for the rest of my life, and I just couldn't stand it. How could this continue to happen over and over again? Was I the avatar in some sinister video game controlled by all the evil forces in the unseen realm?

I reached out to my counselor—the guy I considered to be my pastor—but I couldn't get in touch with him. I immediately sent him a text to tell him what was going on. Maybe he would reach out to my wife and try to intervene with her on my behalf. My son told me he tried to tell her the truth, but she covered his mouth with her hand and said she wouldn't permit him to be influenced to tell a big fat lie just to keep us together. She told him afterward of her plans to divorce me.

He said, "Dad, she's serious about this, and I don't know what to do to change her mind."

I don't guess there was anything anyone could do. She was done! This spiraled me into a state of depression like I have never seen before. I started taking more Hydrocodone than prescribed, which ran me out before my prescription could be refilled. I had made things worse for myself once again. I had eight long, dark, and painful days to go and didn't want to reach out to my cousin again. I hadn't called her for pills in so many years, and I didn't really want to ruin my already damaged testimony to her. I just couldn't be so irresponsible to travel back down that dark and winding road of no return once again. However, I didn't think I could handle the withdrawals either. Maybe these pills wouldn't have the same hellish withdrawal symptoms that I experienced with Oxy.

The next day was okay without my medicine, other than my pain was severe, but I think I could make it seven more days. I was hopefully optimistic, but just when I thought the withdrawals wouldn't affect me, they came like a thief in the night and were so much worse than I remembered them being. I was in nonstop pain and aching everywhere like an abscessed tooth. Thankfully, I didn't have to do an upcoming live stream for the church broadcast this Sunday because we already prerecorded it and had it scheduled to air. I couldn't do anything but vomit, diarrhea in my clothes and all over my bed, and shake uncontrollably from the chills. I thought I was going to die several times and prayed for God to just take me home.

I made it to the third day, which just so happened to be a Sunday. I could barely turn our smart TV on to find the live stream on the Facebook Watch App because I was shaking so violently from the withdrawals. I hadn't heard from my wife or kids in a couple of days. I was at the lowest point I had ever been to. I had plenty of years of experience just staggering through the darkness, but I could've never imagined the depth of the darkness that was my current reality. I lay there in bed, trying to watch myself preach, which wasn't very encouraging. I could understand after watching my own sermon why I never had a big church. Who would want to hear me preach, really? I started to feel sorry for my congregation. Poor folks needed to find someone else and would have a new pastor soon after they boot me out just like the last church when they hear the news of my wife leaving me.

I had succeeded to mess up my marriage, screw up my life, and now my own son is struggling with the same demons as me. I have allowed this curse to be passed down to my own children. I fought a good fight for some time, but it had very few positive results in dispelling the darkness. This darkness would never go away.

I remember reaching over and opening the drawer on the nightstand. I felt around until I located it and could get a firm grip on it and pulled it out of the drawer. It was the Beretta 9 mm that belonged to my daddy at one time, which was still in great condition. I used to call my motorcycle Blue Betsy and decided to name her Black Betsy after all these years. Black Betsy was the only thing that made sense to me at that time, and I just lay there looking at her for what seemed like an hour while I could hear my voice preaching and teaching in the background. I kept saying, "Jesus is better than anything," over and over as I was going through the book of Hebrews.

I managed to get up, stripped the bedding, and put them in the washing machine. I took my ragged T-shirt off and got dressed in my favorite jeans and a new button-up shirt that one of the kids got me for Christmas. I also found my gun cleaning kit and managed to clean Black Betsy. I made sure to leave the kit open on the floor so this would look like an accident. I didn't want life to be tough on my family, and I was worth much more dead than I ever have been or probably would ever be alive.

I placed one hollow point round in the clip and racked the round into the chamber. I pressed the button to release the clip and pointed the gun at my head. So many memories and questions were rushing swiftly through my mind. I wasn't really sure what I believed about suicide. I had read the story of Samson killing the Philistines and himself as he pushed the columns of the palace in, which caused the weight of the structure to come crashing down on all of them, ultimately killing them. I kind of felt like Samson in a way. He could've made much better choices with the God-given strength and abilities he was blessed with, and so could I.

I thought about Ahithophel, Bathsheba's grandpa and King David's counselor. He killed himself. King Saul begged a soldier to kill him while he was injured on the battlefield, which is kinda like killing yourself, right? Judas killed himself, but he is a horrible example to use when you are trying to justify this. I'm sure God will not be pleased with me taking the ending of my life into my own hands, but he is already not pleased with me in so many other areas, so it shouldn't be that big of a deal.

I just kept thinking about my wife and kids. What will they think? I hope my wife uses the insurance policy wisely. I hope her next husband is a better husband and father than me. My family deserves so much more than what they got in me. I wonder if the casket will be open or if there will be too much damage from the gunshot wound to prevent it. I wonder, *Who will preach at my funeral?*

My hand was not steady enough from these wicked withdrawals to attempt to write a farewell note. If I could, I would request my pastor, who started as an acquaintance, turned into my counselor, and ended up being my ministry mentor. He would be able to point my family to Jesus and would comfort them during this tough and confusing time. All of a sudden, I could hear my old man's raspy voice so clearly in my mind, saying, "Really? Are you really gonna blow your frigging brains out with my gun? C'mon, man!" It might seem weird to you, but as soon as he asked this question, I began to laugh hysterically with the gun still pressed tightly to my forehead while the hammer was in the cocked position.

His familiar voice was like a welcome friend even though it was only real in my mind. I answered his question out loud like he was standing in the room engaged in a conversation with me. I said, "Yes, Daddy, I know you probably wouldn't want me to, but it seems like the right thing to do. And I hope it will honor you instead of disgracing you."

I sat down on the side of the bed and placed the gun under my chin. This would probably be a better position to place the barrel in rather than pointing it at my temple. I called my wife and each one of my children's names out individually and told them that I loved them. I spoke blessing and life over them one by one. Afterward, I took a deep breath and pulled the trigger. I did it! I really pulled the trigger! It was a sweet release. If I knew it was going to be this easy, I would've probably killed myself a long time ago. It's all over now, right? Wait a minute! There wasn't any bang, any pain, or any blood. What happened? I could still see. I could still feel my trembling hands holding Black Betsy. I could still hear myself preaching on the television. Maybe the gun jammed?

I began to carefully inspect Black Betsy and could see the hammer in the forward position. The gun didn't appear to be jammed either. I could barely pull the slide back to eject the shell. It looked like I had just pulled it out of the box. There wasn't an imprint from the firing pin on the rim of the shell or on the primer at all. I began to disassemble the gun to see if the firing pin might have fallen out somehow. The firing pin seemed to still be in the correct place. I was extremely confused! I placed the shell back into the magazine, which was lying on the bed beside me, and inserted it forcefully into the old 9 mm. I was not gonna refer to her respectfully as Black Betsy because I was aggravated at her for letting me down. She totally failed me, and I was frustrated with her. I began to coach her into success; it was an intense moment of fellowship, for sure. I could just hear my daddy's laughter in my mind. He always had that wheezing, low-toned, belly laugh that sounded like a wounded duck. He was either making fun of this failed attempt, the confused look on my face, or the fact that his gun wouldn't be the instrument in my self-inflicted death.

Let me just say for the record, guns don't kill people, people kill people, or at least they attempt to when the gun works correctly. It was made for the purpose of firing, right? Not some time but all the time. Maybe Black Betsy was like me, who forfeited the purpose it was created for. I made it to the kitchen and opened the back door. I was so nauseous and sick from the withdrawals. I pulled the slide back again, letting it go to its forward position quickly, which made that unique sound I was so familiar with. The same bullet that misfired earlier was now back in the barrel, and the gun was ready to go. I didn't specifically aim at anything, I just pointed the gun out the kitchen door and pulled the trigger. The gun fired, ejecting the spent casing on the kitchen floor.

The sound was deafening because the muzzle blast was still just barely on the inside of our exterior door, and the smell of gunpowder filled my nostrils as a cool breeze blew through the open door in my direction. Oh my God! It's a real, bona fide miracle! A God moment of supernatural proportions and miraculous magnitude! The shame of my failed suicide attempt engulfed me, but I was really thankful I was alive. My life had been spared! Thank you, Jesus! In that moment of desperation, I took matters into my own hands, kind of like Abraham and Sara did with Hagar when their patience expired. It seemed to make sense at the moment but was incredibly selfish. What was I thinking?

Chapter 11

Making Sense of the Madness

I guess at this time I need to introduce myself. My name is Reggie, and I am the author of this book, well sorta, but the story is not about me. May I explain, please? Thanks! You are awesome! You have been reading the story of Adrian Jay Barber. He actually wrote the book up until now. This was his story, and I promise you that he would be super excited that you have read this far. I will never forget the day we were sitting in my office when he almost started hyperventilating while trying to tell me all about it.

He said, "God has been so good to me as I have staggered through the darkness for most of my life that I have to tell this story. I just gotta write a book."

He was so thankful that God had intervened in such a miraculous way for someone as screwed up as he was. I suggested entitling the book *Staggering through the Darkness*, and he stared at me, almost in a daze, and then sprang out of his seat and gave me a fist bump while saying, "You are a genius, my friend. A genius!"

I was his friend, his pastor, and his counselor, but I don't know about all that genius stuff. My wife would probably disagree with that assessment. I thought it was kind of funny the way he described me in the book, and I really had no idea that he thought so highly of me. I didn't do anything he wouldn't have done for me. Adrian was a great guy and a wonderful father. His kids adored him! I also want to let you know that he was a great preacher, so I can't really agree with his assessment of his preaching ability either.

His wife's name is Mary Jo, and she is an awesome lady, who is so soft-spoken and loves Jesus with all of her heart. Isn't that a sweet, Southern bell kinda name—Mary Jo? She and Adrian, who she also referred to as AJ, were madly in love and had struggles just like most married couples. Their divorce was never finalized, and they were working to reconcile their differences and renew their wedding vows when the accident happened. No, not the motorcycle accident, but the one that ended up taking his life. He made me promise to finish his manuscript if something ever happened to him, so I am doing my best to keep my word to him, my brother-in-arms.

He didn't kill himself. He tried to, but God intervened in a miraculous way. Jesus showed up and showed out right on time. There's no denying it! That moment lit a fire in his soul, and he just knew God spared him to tell his story by writing this book. He never attempted suicide again, which I am aware of, and wanted everyone to know that it's not even a viable solution to any problem someone might be facing. If AJ said it once, he said it one hundred times, "All suicide does is pass the darkness of your worst days onto the people you love the most to scar them permanently for the rest of their lives. Suicide hurts those you love the worst and makes them feel like they weren't enough."

He realized on that dark day, when he attempted to kill himself, that the devil was a liar. He knew this, but he got a greater understanding through his failed suicide attempt. Satan's greater goal in all of our lives is to steal, kill, and destroy. Adrian reached out to Mary Jo, me, and others multiple times that morning but didn't know that his phone died shortly afterward. There were several texts and voicemail messages from me, Mary Jo, and his children. He was losing the battle in his mind, and he was absolutely certain no one really loved him when that was the farthest thing from the truth.

Once I received the second voicemail message from him, I could just hear the distress in his voice, so I drove as hard as I could through two states to pull into the driveway just as he fired Black Betsy out the kitchen door into the backyard. I called him multiple times while I was racing in my truck, just trying to get to him. I've replayed the timeline from that day so many times in my mind. If the gun would've fired the first time he pulled the trigger, I would've been five to ten minutes too late, and he wouldn't have got to spend almost another year with his family and his friends.

It still haunts me as I think about it sometimes. Things would've been different, and you would not be reading his story because this book wouldn't exist. On the other hand, if I got there too early, I would have talked him out of going through with his plans. I had already been down that road with him before, so it was familiar territory. You still wouldn't be reading this book at this time because he would have missed the miracle and would probably still be staggering through the darkness, which is how he would always refer to his life. God worked quickly in that five minutes or so of what I like to call the *in-between time*.

God's timing is so mysterious to me. It always has been. Honestly, my watch and His watch have never really been on the same page. I'm like most selfish people who want things now. I can look back over my life to see those times when God worked slower than I expected and in the in-between times. I would have missed the blessing and the opportunity to grow in faith if it worked any differently. You might be in one of those *in-between times* right now, which could last much longer than five minutes or so.

Let me encourage you to just keep trusting God, friend. He is working even though it might not seem like He is, trust me. So you're probably wondering what happened to him. It was shocking to us all because we knew he was going to change the world because he was so passionate about ministry. Mary Jo said, "Look out, devil, he's gonna put a hurt on the kingdom of darkness," because she had never seen him quite like this before. All of a sudden, like the flip of a switch, my rejoicing turned to mourning when I heard the news.

After the suicide attempt, I took him to the hospital just to make sure he was okay. Later, his primary physician, prescribed some antidepressants. He told him that he would have to be responsible to take them the way they were prescribed because he was already on such strong medication for his pain. Thankfully, they helped to take the edge off his dark plunges to keep him from totally crashing, but he never had a good track record of taking medication the way he was supposed to.

He has been honest about his struggles with me. I am not saying I would have been any better or done things differently. He was already a walking testimony of the grace and power of God by pulling through that motorcycle accident. Medically, he should've been dead a long time ago, but God had other plans. I admired him so much for his grit and determination. He could've just thrown up his hands and quit, but he kept going and was continually in pain. He viewed himself as a *junkie* for so many years, but he wasn't. He was just fighting to survive while trying to live up to everyone's expectations. He was so quick to offer grace to everyone but himself.

When the news spread about his attempted suicide, it caused him some drama at his church, to put it mildly. According to them, "The church really didn't know how to process this information and didn't think he was mentally stable enough to lead the growing congregation." This announcement didn't help his mental health; it totally set him back. Adrian just wanted to serve Jesus ever since that transforming night while his old man, as he called him, was in the intensive care unit. Adrian would tell people later on that he was also in the spiritual ICU; and Dr. Jesus, the Great Physician, delivered him and signed his discharge papers. He was at a low point and took an extra Hydrocodone, which was his fifth one for the day, and two of them in less than two hours, which he unintentionally mixed with two antidepressants his mother gave him. What they didn't know at the time was lethal enough to take his life. She had several prescriptions of Valium all combined into one medication container. She thought she was giving him two capsules of one-milligram benzodiazepine, but she gave him two ten-milligram capsules instead, according to her.

It was just too much at once, which caused an accidental overdose. His mother still deeply grieves over the accident to this day. She blames herself. I couldn't even imagine having to deal with that for the rest of my life. I feel so badly for her. Mary Jo is convinced that she will never marry again. She loved him and left him to try to force him to get some professional help. She always felt like her compassion enabled him to stagger through the darkness. Mary Jo and the kids started attending church services with us again after the funeral. She has just started leading our women's and singles' ministries.

Adrian's eldest son is the drummer in our praise band, and his youngest son just finished launching our church's new website. They are good boys who will make something of themselves by the grace of God. The girls go to the youth ministries and often lead in small groups in Bible devotions. The eldest one looks so much like Adrian, and she is burdened for teens addicted to drugs and who may deal with suicidal thoughts. The whole family has been such a blessing to our church family, and all of them miss Brother Adrian. Adrian would be so proud of his family. I preached at his funeral and entitled the message, "Staggering through the Darkness." I thought it was a fitting title for his memorial service. It was raw and real.

I told his story, he would have wanted me to. The church he was ministering at during the time of his death has already gone through another pastor and is currently on the hunt again for someone to lead them. My biggest regret in all of this was recommending him to that church even though God used him greatly during the time he served there. They were too focused on keeping their church the way it had been for the past fifty years and resisted growth, which they called "unnecessary change."

Not all change is bad even though some churches view it as a compromise or maybe even as a cussword. Adrian, along with so many other pastors, knew this all too well. If you have learned anything from Adrian's story, I hope you can see how God chooses to use imperfect people to accomplish great things. Life is messy. Ministry is messy. There aren't any perfect people on this earth, and neither are there any perfect ministries. Guess what? Your church isn't perfect either, and neither is mine because you are imperfect, and so am I. I hope you will also see the importance of giving yourself some grace. Guilt and shame gripped Adrian's life. He would repent and then continue to wrestle with guilt. We need to realize and distinguish between the voice of conviction that comes from the still, small voice of the Holy Spirit and the voice of condemnation that comes from Satan, our enemy.

He wants to convince us of our guilt after God cleanses us to trick us into thinking differently about ourselves than the way God truly sees us. This renders us helpless and defeated on the battlefield in our minds. God's Word is more authoritative than your feelings. We need to constantly remind ourselves that faith is greater than fear, and faith is also greater than the way we feel even about ourselves. Remember, you are the imago Dei, an image bearer of the divine. If you have a relationship with Jesus, you are so much more than just an image bearer. You are part of the family as an adopted child of the King. Jesus bore the sins and shame of the entire world and willingly took God's wrath being poured out on him instead of me and you. God must punish sin, not just because He is holy but because He graciously pardons and justifies sinners through Jesus.

This is how God the Father enlarges the family. He wants us all to be His children and feast continually at His table of grace. As we fight our spiritual battles, He continually fights for us if we will let him. When we sin, he will forgive us because we are his children. Adrian tried to walk in forgiveness, but the voice of condemnation convinced him to remain in the bondage he created for himself. He realized this after God kept his handgun from firing and made great strides in the little time he had left.

Please hear me out on this. Let me share Adrian's heart. Turn up the volume and pump up the jam for just a minute. Adrian would want you to know that suicide is never the answer! Please don't hurt yourself and those you love. That was the main reason he wanted to write this book, to tell you his story. You are fearfully and wonderfully made with a divine purpose, which was assigned to you by your Creator. God is the giver and the taker of life. If you're still breathing, there's still hope for you. Talk to somebody, please! Your family and friends would rather listen to your failures, flaws, and heartaches than attend your funeral. I promise!

Adrian never chose to be addicted to prescription narcotics, just like millions of other Americans. The opioid epidemic has been a curse perpetrated on our society by Big Pharma, in my opinion. Prescription narcotic addiction is not only dangerous, but I have seen it lead to so many other lethal drugs, like heroin and meth. I am convinced that opioids are gateway drugs, not because of some scientific data but because I have witnessed the broken pieces of one shattered life after the other, in the heart of the Bible Belt, where there's a church on every corner. There are so many people just like Adrian. What a shame! Please follow the advice of your doctor when taking prescription narcotics and don't wait to reach out for help if you or someone you love is negatively affected by any medication.

Another wicked curse that continues to ruin and wreck lives is pornography. It might just be Satan's most successful tool ever employed to exploit innocence, kill intimacy in a marriage, and destroy families. Every day, another little kid, intentionally or accidentally, looks at another unwholesome pic or video for the first time; and it changes them forever with just one look. They will never be the same as they are now at war in their still-developing minds but do not have the weapons or the necessary skills to even put up a fight.

The hook has been set because the lure is so attractive. Their curiosity continues to get the best of them, and they conduct another search even though they know it's wrong. Before they even know it, their cravings get the best of them as they want more and more on this unstoppable smut journey.

I just spoke with one of my friends in the ministry who made this statement to me over a hot cup of coffee: "Porn is the worst problem the church has ever faced, and it's getting worse. Teenagers today don't even see it as immoral. They think not recycling is worse than viewing pornography. We are totally desensitized to it as more than one million people are viewing porn every minute in America."

I almost got strangled as the harsh reality of what he was saying hit me as I took a big drink of my Folgers Dark Silk blend. Please seek out professional help if you are struggling with porn addiction. You are not alone, and you are not doomed! You can get victory over pornography through the power of the gospel, counseling, and plenty of accountability. Please stop hiding and keeping these secrets that are eating away at your soul. Tell a trusted friend or a pastor or call one of the many porn addiction hotlines to take the first step on your road to recovery today.

I remember just sitting in my office with that knot stuck in my throat and tears filling my eyes as Adrian opened up to me about his experience with his middle-school teacher. It was one of the most heartbreaking stories I ever heard or probably ever will hear. I don't know if he ever truly was able to heal from the trauma this caused him. He continued to carry it around with him like an open wound he ignored. I asked him if he thought a lot of what he endured was the ugly side effects of not dealing with such painful trauma at such an early age.

He said, "Nope, I am not making excuses or blame-shifting. What she did was wrong, but it didn't make me who I am."

I appreciated his resilience, but I don't know if I agreed with him. Furthermore, I certainly did not agree with his silence and encouraged him to speak out. He refused to but told me he would pray about writing about it in this book even though he really didn't want to. He felt like by retelling his story, he would endure more trauma. Adrian really didn't want to have to sift through such painful memories to relive those moments over again. It was easier for him to attempt to tuck it away, but it certainly wasn't healthy.

If you are a victim of sexual abuse, please speak out and tell someone. Adrian would give you the same advice, but he just couldn't bring himself to follow through personally on exposing his perpetrator. I told him that he had spent years protecting the woman who exploited his innocence, and it just isn't right to offer her that kind of protection. He would say, "Okay, Reg, time for another cup of coffee." This was his way of transitioning to something else and sidestepping the big issue, like a matador barely escaping the blitz of a raging bull at the last second.

Pastor, preacher, and minister, if you are reading this book, please quit trying to be Superman. You were created for community and you—yes, even you—need help from people just as much as you want to help people. If you are struggling, just don't keep staggering through the darkness like Adrian did. It seems like every day, I hear of another ministry leader who has left the ministry, receives divorce papers, or commits suicide. Don't try to fight your battles alone. Speak up, be honest, and get help. We need your light now more than ever as this world continues to get darker and more dangerous. We can't afford to lose one more leader in the Body of Christ. Somebody is counting on you to do what God has called you to do today. It might not seem like it, but you are making a difference. You don't have to be perfect; I know you want to be, and I cling to the promise that you will be in heaven, but you can't be down here. I hope the Body of Christ will one day give you as much grace as you have given them over the years even though we are held to a higher standard—may it be a biblical standard.

If you are new to the kingdom, you need to know that your pastoral staff, as well as all those who serve in the ministry, can get stressed out and may need a day off from time to time. Believe it or not, we work more than just a couple of hours one day per week. We also have financial needs just like you do and have seasons where extra money seems extremely hard to come by. We have bad days and fall into sin just like you but seldom have anyone we can talk to about our struggles for fear of people walking out of our lives.

Adrian had helped so many people, but he felt alone when he needed help the most. This wasn't true, so many people loved him deeply, but perception is often reality, right? Our spiritual foe wants to make us feel like we are alone. This is where he begins his greatest assault on the battlefield of our minds. A banana can't get peeled unless it gets isolated from the bunch, right? Satan wants to make us feel alone and isolated so he can sew his sinister seeds of doubt and worthlessness into our minds.

Hopefully, we are walking in repentance, renewing our minds daily, and have a good accountability team around us, like a group of bananas. If you are struggling with porn, prescription medication addiction, or anything else, may the church of Jesus Christ love you where you are and walk with you into freedom. I promise you by the authority of the holy scriptures and personal testimony, you can be set free. Salvation, through the glorious gospel of Jesus, is the good news you need to hear. I know you may know it like the front and back of your dominant hand, but is it still transforming you? Never forget that the same gospel, which was powerful enough to save you, is the only transforming power in your life. You continually need it and will never graduate from it.

Biblical salvation or the kind that makes you righteous, holy, accepted by God, and a citizen of Heaven is more than fire insurance. It is a moment of repentance and faith that leads to a life of faith over fear, cross-bearing discipleship, and more repentance as you are continually conformed to the image of Christ through sanctification. Adrian would want you to know that there will never be anything you face in this life more powerful than the resurrection of Jesus.

If you happen to be staggering through the darkness right now, don't stop. Keep on walking, but just turn quickly and continue your walk in the opposite direction. The faintest glimmer of light can dispel the most frightening darkness. May the real and raw story of Adrian Jay Barber—a man who understood the darkness but found hope in the light of Jesus—be encouraging to you as it shines a little light in your darkness. Even though he's gone, he's not dead. He's shining brighter than he ever thought he could in that perfect place, where no one is staggering through the darkness, because darkness doesn't exist there.

I'm going to give Adrian the final word. It's the right thing to do because it's his story. Bits and pieces of it might even closely resemble your story. It probably does. I really don't know if this was his vision for the end of this book, but Mary Jo gave me her stamp of approval, which was good enough for me. Here is an entry from one of his journals. I keep it in my Bible and read it often to remind me of my living hope and to intentionally be a ray of light in a world of darkness.

> I can't even see with my eyes wide open. How is that possible? Oh yeah, I know, it's the darkness. My old friend, just like the familiar lyrics to the song by Simon and Garfunkel. The only constant thing in my crazy life is darkness. It's so deceptive and yet becomes painfully comfortable so quickly. Will it ever vanish? Will it ever lift? Will my eyes ever be able to readjust

to the light? Is light even real or just a figment of my imagination? These were the questions that plagued my mind for years and led me to stagger through more darkness. Oh, Lord, just when it seemed like the darkness was the darkest it had ever been, your glorious light sprung in and invaded my darkness. What a difference your light truly makes. My heart's desire and ultimate goal is to be the reflection of your light in the darkness. Make me your instrument, the vessel that carries your light, no matter what it may cost me. Break me in however many pieces you desire, no matter how painful it may be, so your light may penetrate the darkness through my pain. If it lasts more than 1,000 years, it will be worth it because you are worth it and so much more, King Jesus, my light in the darkness.

About the Author

R. J. Tipton has been married for more than twenty years to his high school sweetheart. He is the father of five incredible children and the friend of a micro goldendoodle named Moses. "Bro. Reg," as he is called, has been in ministry since 1998 and serves as the senior/lead pastor of the Hill Church in Liberty, Kentucky—a church he planted and organized during the coronavirus pandemic in 2020. He is also the principal of the Galilean Christian Academy, a private Christian school, which is also located in Liberty, Kentucky.